SCOTT BURTON ON THE RANGE

By *EDWARD G. CHEYNEY*

Presented by ithink books

ithinkbooks@gmail.com

...

TABLE OF CONTENTS

CHAPTER I
INTO A FAR COUNTRY

Scott Burton leaned eagerly forward and searched the scenery which rolled steadily past the Pullman window. The other occupants of the car, worn out with the long journey and surfeited with scenery, centered their attention on their books or tried to sleep away the weary miles. They had seen it all, or at least too much of it. But to Scott Burton it was a new country and to him a new country was of more absorbing interest than anything else.

Born in a little Massachusetts town, he had lived a stay at home life with the single exception of his trip to a college in the Middle West. But even then, before he had any idea that he would ever really have a chance to travel, it was always the tales of strange lands that fascinated him. He had been looking out of that car window for three solid days just as intently as he was looking now and there was not a bump on the landscape which failed to interest him. He had laid over one night in St. Louis that he might not miss anything by night travel, and another one in Pueblo. And still he stared at the country with almost unwinking eye.

A kindly old gentleman who had been watching him for some time, and whose curiosity was piqued by the boy's unusual alertness, dropped into the seat beside him and opened a conversation.

"Pardon me," he said. "Tell me if I annoy you, but it hurts my eyes to read on the train, I have seen the country no end of times and I can't sleep in the daytime. That leaves me nothing to do but watch my neighbors; and I have been watching you till I could not keep down my curiosity any longer."

Scott was glad to have some one to talk to and he liked the old man's manner. Moreover, he felt rather curious to know what had made the other man curious.

"I suppose I am rather curious looking," Scott laughed.

"No, no," protested the old gentleman, "that is a very good pun, but it is not at all what I meant."

"I did not mean it either," said Scott, "I shall be very glad of your company, especially if you have seen the country so often."

"Well," said the old gentleman, hastening to satisfy his curiosity, "I have been watching you stare out of that window for almost a whole day now, and I simply could not wait any longer to learn what you were hunting for."

"I am afraid it will be horribly disappointing to you," Scott smiled, "but I am only looking at the country."

"Looking at the country," the old man echoed, "all day long." He seemed not only disappointed but also a little incredulous.

"Why, yes," Scott said, "you see it is all new to me."

"I don't see what there is in this country that a man would want to look at for a whole day," the old man insisted.

"But I have never seen a mountain before," Scott answered, "and right over there is the Great Divide. I have always been crazy to see a mountain."

"They are a grand sight," said the old gentleman. "Those old peaks up there are like brothers to me. Yes, they must look pretty fine to a stranger. They look pretty good to me when I have been away for a while. Mountains are a good deal like home folks, you don't think much about them when you are with them all the time, but when you go away you are crazy to get back to them."

"You live here then?" Scott asked politely.

"Live here," exclaimed the old man indignantly, "wouldn't live anywhere else. I reckon I have been living here longer than most anything else except those old mountains there. Why, I used to start out at the Mexican border with a herd of cattle every spring and graze 'em right north to Montana in time for the fall market. Right straight through we drove 'em and never seen a settler the whole summer. I knew every water hole from the Big Bend to Miles City."

"I've read about that," said Scott becoming really interested. "It must have been great sport."

"Sport! You bet it was. And there was money in cattle, too, in the good old days before the settler and the sheep men came. Can't chase a jack rabbit now," he added a little bitterly, "without scratching your horse's nose on a barbed wire fence."

"Don't the cattle men make any money now?" Scott asked.

"Some, but it's mostly sheep in here now. Had to go into sheep myself," he grinned. "I fought 'em for a long time but I saw it wasn't any use, so I bought some myself, and I've made my pile out of 'em. There's some that's fighting them yet, but they'll never get anywhere."

"I suppose you had some pretty bitter fights," Scott said encouragingly.

"I should remark. When I went into sheep, all the cattle men looked on me as a traitor. The sheep men were mostly greasers then and I was one of the first white men in this section to go into it. I remember when I rode up from San Rosario with my first band of sheep and met old Tom Butler on the plain he tried to pull his gun on me, but I had the drop on him and I made him set there while I told him what I thought of the situation. He did a lot of cussin' and spittin', but it soaked into him all right and when I beat him onto the summer range in the spring, he sold out his cattle and bought him a band of sheep. That's where we had the fights, for the summer range, up there on those old mountains."

The old man looked dreamily toward the towering mountains and Scott knew that he was living over a story that would be good to hear.

"You had to race for the summer range, didn't you?" he asked.

"Race for it? Lord, yes! The whole caboodle of us would live as peaceable as a bunch of kittens down on the plains all winter, but when spring was coming we all got sort of offish and nervous. Each man was scared to start too early for fear there would not be any feed in the mountains, and he was scared to wait too long for fear the other fellow would beat him to it. I remember one time when old Tim Murphy tied a sheep bell on his dog and led him by old José's place in the night going towards the mountains. It was two weeks sooner than any one would have dared to move, but José was so scared that he started his whole band before daylight and drove 'em ten miles before he found out that Tim had fooled him."

"I suppose the government regulation of the range has spoiled all that now?" Scott suggested.

"Spoiled it!" the old man exclaimed, "Yes, they've spoiled it, and it's a mighty good thing, too. There were lots of lambs lost in that spring race for the grass, many an acre of range spoiled, and many a small rancher ruined. Even when you succeeded in beating the other fellow to the range you never knew how long it would be 'til some bigger fellow would come along and crowd you off. Now you know a year ahead just what you are going to get, how many head you can hold over, and that the grass will be there whenever you want to go."

"But I thought the sheep men were opposed to the government regulation," Scott protested.

"Humph," grunted the old man contemptuously, "some of 'em are. They are the fellows who want to hog the whole thing and crowd out the little fellow. The government will not let them do that and they are sore. Still think they are bigger than Uncle Sam. I knew better right from the first and took my medicine like a man and now I like it."

"It is certainly building up the range," Scott said; "they are supporting more sheep now than under the old system and doing it better."

"Certainly they are," agreed the old gentleman. "You seem to know a good deal about this country, young man, for any one who has never seen a mountain before," he added suspiciously.

Scott laughed. "I don't know nearly as much about it as I should like to. I have been reading up on it because I am coming down here to work, but it seems as though the very things a fellow wants to know most are always left out of the books."

"What are you going to do, if it is any of my business?"

"It may be some of your business," Scott laughed. "I'm going to be a patrolman with the Forest Service."

"On what forest?"

"The Cormorant."

"No, too far west, you will not get any of mine there. You don't know the west at all?" he asked musingly.

"Only what I have read," Scott said. "I feel as though I know the timber pretty well, but I'm afraid I don't know the stock business at all."

"Well, I'm leaving you at the next station. I get over your way once in a while and shall probably see you again, if you stay there," he added with a grin. "If you study the stock business the way you have been studying this country, and keep your eye on Jed Clark you will be all right. Don't let them bluff you." With this advice he walked back to his seat to collect his things.

Scott turned back to his examination of the country, but his mind was busy with the old man's last remarks. He had intimated that patrolmen did not last very long in that particular section, and had warned him specifically against one man. Evidently some of the former patrolmen had been bluffed out. Well, he was willing to admit that he was a tenderfoot with very little knowledge of the stock business, but he made up his mind right there that no one was going to bluff him. He did not believe in going out to meet trouble, but he never dreamed how often the old man's advice would stand him in good stead. Possibly if he had, he would have thought about it a little longer.

The train skirted the edges of queer, flat-topped mesas which appeared to be scattered carelessly about the plain; timber crowned and green they were in the midst of the dark brown of the dried up plains. Gradually the great mountains were closing in. Irregular saw-tooth ranges took the place of the mesas, deep-cut gulches caused the track to make long detours— twenty miles in one place—to get a mile across a ravine. Far down in one of the narrow valleys he saw a flock of sheep, the first time in his life he had ever seen more than twenty-five in any one bunch.

He was now rapidly approaching the little town which was to be his headquarters. As the train rounded the shoulder of a mountain which jutted out into the valley, he saw it afar off. It looked very small and insignificant in the center of that great flat plain, and also very bare and treeless to a lad from a superbly elm-clad New England village. And all about it the baked plain lay glaring in the late afternoon sun. It seemed a queer place to pick for a town, but it was just like most of the others he had seen in the last two hundred miles.

On either side of the plain, apparently walling it in with an unbroken rim, were the mountains. In the clear atmosphere they seemed to rise sheer from the valley like perpendicular walls. On them the pine forests were draped like a mantle hanging down toward the valley in irregular points and fringes, and between these points like great wedges driven up into the slope from the valley, were triangular patches of aspen marking the cañons.

At long intervals slender green threads extending down from the larger cañons to the wiggling green line in the center of the plain traced the more or less permanent water courses. It did not look very attractive to Scott and he scanned the mountains with a good deal of satisfaction in the thought that most of his work would be up there.

Scott was the only passenger to get off the train at the little town. He was thoroughly inspected by the station loafers as he shouldered his packsack and started boldly up the main street, almost the only street in the town. Like so many western towns it was built like a string of beads. To Scott's eastern eyes the mixture of little 'dobe houses, concrete block stores, cement sidewalks and electric street lights presented a strange mixture. The complete absence of trees and the consequent glare of light almost blinded him, it was such a contrast to the darkened elm-lined streets of his old home town.

Scott did not see how he could very well get lost in a one-street town. He trudged along as though he had known the place for years and carefully inspected each building for some sign of the supervisor's office. In the fourth block he found it. The Stars and Stripes waving from the roof caught his attention and painted on the second story window he saw the sign, "Cormorant National Forest, Supervisor's Office."

He ascended the stairs rather nervously, for he was entering upon his first real job, and upon entering the office found himself confronted by the clerk. The clerk sized him up, guessed who he was, but remained contemptuously silent. It was the contempt of a native son for an Eastern man.

"Mr. Ramsey?" Scott asked.

"In the next room," growled the clerk, nodding toward an open door.

Scott dropped his packsack in a corner and walked in, curious to see what his chief would be like. He was surprised to see a man who looked little older than himself. He was dark, of middle height, broad shouldered and square of jaw. Scott noted the straight cut, thin lipped mouth and was not very favorably impressed. Here would be a hard, unsympathetic man to deal with. The supervisor looked up at the sound of his step and the clear frank look reassured him a little.

"Mr. Ramsey?" Scott inquired again.

"Yes," said the supervisor quietly.

"My name is Burton. I have been assigned to this forest and ordered to report to you."

The supervisor smiled cordially and lost his "hard" look at once. "I am glad to meet you, Mr. Burton," he said, rising to shake hands. "I have been expecting you and hoping that you would come to-day. It is almost time for the range to open up and we need you badly." He closed the door into the outer office. "I know that you have just landed from a long trip and are probably tired, but there are one or two things that I want to tell you now. It may save you trouble later. Have a seat."

Scott was a little surprised at being pushed into the harness so soon, but he was anxious to get to work, and the town, as he had seen it, did not seem to offer any attractions. He sat down to get his first instructions.

"I'll be perfectly frank with you," said Mr. Ramsey, "because if we are going to get along together we have to understand each other. The job to which you have been assigned is a hard and not altogether pleasant one. The three men who have held it have been busted out one after the other in rapid succession because they have either been 'run out' or 'bought up' by the sheep men. The regulations are to be enforced in that district." His face looked hard enough now. "It is the only district in this forest where they have not always been enforced in the past and I am going to put them through there if I have to bust a patrolman every week to do it."

"You will have a particularly hard time because you are an Easterner. These Westerners will all look on you with contempt until you make good and will try to slip something over on you at every opportunity. As a rule, we do not put an Easterner in as a patrolman for that reason. But since the last man there seemed to be in the pay of the sheep men as well as of the service I determined to try an Eastern man who would be a stranger here."

"I am afraid it will be only too plain that I am not connected with the sheep men," Scott laughed. "I am horribly green on the sheep business."

"I am glad of it," Mr. Ramsey replied. "Don't let any of these fellows here in town get you into a muss before you get out of town. They will probably try it. They will guy you at every opportunity. Take it as well as you can, but do not let any one walk over you."

"Thank you," Scott said, "I appreciate your advice and shall try to keep out of trouble."

The quiet answer which showed neither boastfulness nor a willingness to be walked over seemed to please the supervisor. "Good," he exclaimed, "now I'll take you over to the hotel and you can get some supper and a little rest. To-morrow we'll get you outfitted, and the next day I'll take you out to your headquarters and show you around a little."

Mr. Ramsey introduced Scott to the clerk, Mr. Benson. The clerk shook hands grouchily, and Scott understood that his reports and expense accounts would have to be flawless if they were to get by this man who seemed to have conceived a violent dislike for him at first sight. If he could have seen him a few minutes before listening at the keyhole he would have been even more certain of it.

The supervisor led the way up the street to a very comfortable looking up-to-date hotel. Nearly every one spoke pleasantly to the supervisor but looked Scott over with a rather amused and condescending smile. One man especially, whom they passed just outside of the hotel, stared at Scott with a malicious sneer of contempt that was hard to overlook; nor did he make any pretense of speaking to Mr. Ramsey.

In the hotel Scott was introduced to Mr. McGoorty, the proprietor. "Put him in the boys' room, McGoorty," the supervisor explained. "He is one of the new patrolmen and will probably be in from time to time like the rest of them. Well, so long, Burton. McGoorty will take care of you. Come over in the morning at about eight."

At the door he turned back suddenly and spoke to Scott aside. "Did you notice that sour looking fellow just outside?"

"Yes, I wanted to punch him."

"Don't do it. That is Jed Clark, the worst sheep man in the country. He is probably in town now to size you up. He seems to get all the news somehow. Don't mix with him, no matter what happens."

Scott was not sure that he could resist it if he had another of those sneering looks, and as he went up to his room he heard several uncomplimentary remarks which made his blood boil. "These Westerners may be hospitable and warm hearted," he muttered to himself, "but they have a mighty peculiar way of showing it."

Edward G. Cheyney

CHAPTER II
SCOTT GETS ACQUAINTED WITH JED CLARK

Scott came down to breakfast early. He wanted to be on time at the office, but his real reason was to try to dodge some of his numerous critics. He was only partially successful, for there were several others in the dining room, and he caught scraps of conversation followed by loud laughs which were so evidently meant for his ears that it was hard to ignore them. He was almost at the end of his patience, and was glad when the time came to go to the office.

The grouchy clerk was just coming in when Scott arrived, but the supervisor was hard at work and had been for an hour. He greeted Scott briskly. "Good morning," he looked at Scott keenly. "Have you been able to hold onto yourself?"

"So far," Scott answered and added doggedly, "but I can't keep it up much longer. The sooner I get into the brush the better."

"Maybe you are right," said the supervisor thoughtfully. "If we can get hold of a good pony this morning maybe we can start after dinner."

"That will suit me," Scott said. "I don't want to start life here with a fight but a man cannot stand this kind of thing forever."

"Then we will get out as soon as possible," said the supervisor with decision. "Jed Clark and his crowd would like nothing better than to get you into a fight."

"Then why not have it and get it over with?" Scott asked. He had been the champion boxer at college, and had many an hour's training from an old ex-prize fighter in his father's stable. He was not naturally pugnacious, but he felt confident that he could give a good account of himself and the prospect of a fight did not worry him.

"That would work all right," said the supervisor smiling, "if they fought your way, but they don't. They fight with guns in this country. They figure that you know nothing about that and would make you ridiculous if you started anything. That's what they want."

Scott had not thought of that. He could see now why Mr. Ramsey had been so anxious to keep him out of a mix-up. He had never handled a pistol, had never dreamed of shooting a man, and was somewhat dazed by this new situation.

The supervisor saw his predicament and came to his rescue. "Have you the money in hand to buy a horse and an outfit?" he asked, "or will we have to buy it on 'tick'?"

"I have three hundred dollars," Scott answered absently, still preoccupied with the gun problem.

"Oh, I guess that will be enough," the supervisor laughed. "Let's go down to the corral and see what they have there in the way of horse flesh."

They started for the horse corral which was far out at one end of town. The supervisor seemed a little thoughtful and they walked a block in silence.

"Do you ride?" he asked suddenly as though following out his own train of thought.

"Farm horses," Scott replied. "I have never tried any bucking bronchos."

Again the supervisor was thoughtful. "They never expect an Eastern man to know how to ride," he said. "They will have every bucking skate in the country down there this morning and the boys will all be out to see you thrown."

Scott's jaw squared perceptibly but he said nothing.

The supervisor misunderstood his silence and glanced at him out of the corner of his eye. "Perhaps I can try them out for you and you can try one later when there are not so many spectators."

"Thanks," Scott said, "that is very kind of you, and I do need your judgment in picking a good one, for I do not know very much about a horse myself, but I think that I had better do the riding. They will probably throw me all right but I do not like the idea of side-stepping it."

The supervisor looked relieved. "Oh, they don't all buck. The bad ones are pretty well known and I can warn you off of them. The cowboys do not like a bucking horse any better than you do except to play with."

They reached the corral and as the supervisor had predicted there was a good gallery to see the green-horn spilled. There was also in the corral the finest collection of outlaws that the supervisor had ever seen there. Jed Clark had attended to that personally.

They leaned on the fence and looked the bunch over. Some were old and broken-down plugs, worn out with long service; others were strong enough, but the most of them were Roman-nosed, spike-eared, wild-eyed fellows marked with the scars of many battles. They trotted restlessly about the corral and kept a wary eye on any movement which might indicate the throwing of a rope.

"Don't think much of any of them," Mr. Ramsey said, after making a careful survey of the bunch. "They are all either skates or outlaws."

Scott had been perfectly truthful when he had said that he did not know much about horses. In fact he did not know anything at all about these bronchos. None of the signs which any plainsman could read like a book meant anything to him. But he did have an eye for beauty and there was one horse in that drove which had fascinated him at first glance.

Coal black, with a shiny velvet coat which glistened in the sunshine, his shapely head held high on a gracefully arching neck, he seemed the very essence of grace. He kept a little apart from the drove but was evidently their acknowledged leader. He kept almost continually on the go except when he paused momentarily to scan some movement outside the fence. There was a certain royal dignity in all his graceful movements, and a scorn of man in his every glance. Scott knew at once that he would have that horse regardless of cost or expert advice to the contrary. He had been surprised at the supervisor's comment but supposed it was just part of the horse dealer's stock in trade.

"Isn't that black a beauty?" he whispered.

"Keep off of him," the supervisor warned. "He belongs to Jed Clark and is the wildest in the bunch. Nobody has ever ridden him and Jed would not sell him for a thousand dollars. He only put him in here to try to kill you. He certainly is a beauty, though."

"Why haven't they ridden him?" Scott asked, curious but not discouraged.

"Well, Jed just keeps him for breeding and he is so wild that even the cowboys are half afraid of him. He killed a man once. That sorrel over there looks like the best buy to me."

"How much do they want for him?" Scott asked absently.

"How much for the sorrel, Mose?" the supervisor asked of the man who was in charge of the corral.

"Sixty dollars," Mose grunted indifferently. A general look of disappointment passed over the crowd, for if Scott bought the sorrel there would be no show for them.

"Not the sorrel," Scott said, "I meant the black." The crowd perked up and nudged each other expectantly.

"Sixty-five dollars," Mose answered with the same indifference; but the crowd held its breath. The supervisor looked at Scott curiously.

"I'll take him," Scott said with as much indifference as he could assume. He was really so excited that he could hardly talk. It seemed to him that there never had been anything which he wanted quite as badly as he wanted that horse. Jed Clark started up and waited anxiously with the others for the answer to the next question.

"Want to ride him home?" Mose drawled.

The supervisor listened anxiously along with the others. The situation had passed beyond his control. He knew that it would be extremely foolhardy for Scott, ignorant of Western horses as he was, to tackle that untamed, beautiful brute. It might mean serious injury, it would certainly keep him off of the job for a few days at a time when he was badly needed, and yet the supervisor knew that he would like Scott better if he accepted the challenge and fought it out before them all. If he did not attempt to ride the horse he had bought he would be generally branded as a coward, even by many men who would not dare try it themselves, but if he took his chance he would make a substantial advance in the appreciation of the community no matter how poor an exhibition he made.

"I'll ride him if I can borrow a saddle and bridle," Scott replied without the least hesitation. The crowd heaved a sigh of relief and Jed Clark settled comfortably back against the fence with a wink at his neighbor.

"Saddle him up, will you, Jed?" Mose called without changing his position or interrupting his conversation.

Jed was the only man in the country who could put his hand on that beautiful stallion without using a rope and there were very few who could rope him. He had taught him that as a colt but he had never tried to ride him. "Is the undertaker here?" he whispered to one of his friends as he climbed leisurely into the corral. The other horses dashed wildly into the opposite corner, but the big black stood his ground and watched his approaching master with head high and sensitive nostrils aquiver. He lowered his head a little condescendingly when Jed patted his shiny neck, took a lump of sugar with great relish, and allowed himself to be bridled without any objection. He was used to that. He followed along quietly enough when Jed led him over to the fence, and picked up a light English saddle, carefully wrapped in a blanket and slipped it gently over his back. Jed buckled the girth and whispered to one of his admirers, "He thinks it's just a blanket, he's used to that."

"All right, you," he called to Scott as he led the horse back to the middle of the corral.

The supervisor was just giving Scott a little final advice. "Don't monkey with him any more than you have to before you get on, it makes 'em nervous. Walk right up, put your foot square in the stirrup, mount as quickly as you can without a jerk, be sure to catch the second stirrup, and hold on tight with your knees. Never let him see you hesitate or think that you are afraid of him."

"I'll do the best I can," Scott replied quietly, "but I do not suppose that I can stay on long," and he started to climb the fence.

Just then the supervisor caught sight of the English saddle. "Hold on there, Jed," he called angrily, "what kind of a saddle is that for a bucking broncho?"

"It's an English saddle and your friend's English, ain't he?" Jed sneered. It was a brilliant retort but it did not bring the response that he expected except from a few of his friends.

"I don't care what nationality he is," responded the supervisor resolutely. "I don't want to spoil your fun, but I am not going to stand here and see one of my men murdered. There is not a cowboy in this crowd who would try to ride that horse with that saddle and you know it."

There was a murmur of approval from the crowd. They were perfectly willing to see Scott spilled, had come there for that particular purpose, but they wanted fair play and an English saddle was no saddle at all in their eyes. Mr. Ramsey was right when he said that none of them would have used it. There is nothing for which a cowboy has more genuine contempt than for an English saddle. Jed was embarrassed by the decided disfavor of the crowd where he had expected unanimous support, but he stood his ground doggedly.

"That ain't no fair game, Jed," Mr. McGoorty, the hotel keeper and mayor of the town called from the fence, "and you ain't goin' to boost no greenhorn onto that fingernail affair in this town with my consent."

"Mack's scared he's goin' to lose a boarder," Mose drawled.

The controversy bid fair to become serious with the odds very much against Jed Clark when Scott unexpectedly brought it to an abrupt termination. "That is the only kind of saddle I have ever used," he said, "and I might as well try it. He can't throw me much farther out of that than he could out of the other kind."

He walked quietly up to the horse behind Jed, who was facing his opponents, grasped the reins firmly, and before any one realized what he was doing he was squarely astride the big black. A sudden stillness fell upon the crowd. Jed Clark, seeing what had happened, made a wild dash for the fence. He had enjoyed posing as the only man who could pet that beautiful wild animal, but he had no desire to be within reach when the royal beauty learned of the indignity which had been put upon him. Scott felt just as he had many a time before when he had put on the gloves with a man who, he knew, could outbox him. He had no hope of success but was determined to do his best. He had never seen a Western horse perform and did not fully realize the seriousness of the situation.

For a moment the great horse stood dazed and puzzled by this new burden. He had never had any experience in throwing a man; no man had ever before presumed to burden him. He moved nervously and Scott's tightening knees drove terror and rage to his very heart. He forgot the inherited secret of his race;

he forgot the wily strategy he had often seen his fellows use to such good purpose; it never occurred to him to buck. He wanted only to get away, to be rid of that devil on his back. With a mighty bound he started at full speed for the six foot fence around the corral, his eyes flaring and his nostrils distended with abject terror. The supervisor's heart sank as the maddened brute, blinded with rage approached the barrier. Then there arose a gasp of mingled astonishment and admiration as the great horse, heedless of the scattering crowd, rose to the fence like a bird, cleared it by a wide margin, and tore away down the main street. There was a great scurrying among the spectators to get their saddle horses for the pursuit, but every one knew that there was not another horse in the country which could compare with Jed Clark's stallion for speed, and long before any of the cowboys had mounted, the black had cleared the east end of the town leaving a train of staring excited faces behind him.

It was by the merest chance that Scott had been able to stick on when his horse had jumped the high fence. He had been leaning too far forward and had received a tremendous blow on the nose from the horse's head. Nothing but his boxing experience prevented him from going off. He had learned to keep his balance for an instant even when completely stunned. He recovered quickly from the blow and found himself clinging tightly to the horse's mane as the hazy houses whisked past on either side. Then he shot out into the open plain and the wind roared in his ears. It did not seem to Scott as though he had ever traveled as fast before even in an automobile.

The rush of the wind soon cleared his brain and with his returning senses he regained his nerve which the unexpected blow had badly shattered. He did not know whether the horse had jumped over the fence, something that did not seem possible, or through it. At any rate this was lots better than bucking. His stirrups were too long and bothered him, but he was beginning to feel that he might stay on if the horse did not do anything but run. Surely no horse could keep up that pace long and he might be manageable when he was tired out.

But he had not counted on the wonderful endurance of a range-bred stallion which ran almost as much as he walked. Mile after mile his mighty strides carried him over the sun-baked plain. Scott looked back toward the town and saw a few specks in the distance, hard riding cowboys doing their best but falling hopelessly behind. "If he keeps this up for an hour," Scott thought, "and then throws me, it will take me a week to walk back." Ten miles of plain separated them from the town and the steady pounding of his hoofs was still as rhythmical as clock work.

"Oh, you beautiful wonder!" Scott exclaimed aloud in affectionate tones and stroked the glossy neck while he still held onto the mane with his other hand. "I would not trade you for all the others in the corral even if I never learn to ride you."

The gentle voice and the stroking had produced a peculiar effect on the maddened horse. The rushing wind and the freedom of his movements—for Scott had not attempted even to hold onto the reins—had somewhat restored his shattered nerves and soothed his injured dignity. He had been expecting something terrible to happen and instead a kindly voice had spoken to him and a gentle hand had stroked his neck. It had usually meant sugar for him and no harm had ever come of it. The madness slowly left his eyes and his pace slackened to an easy lope, a trot and then he stopped in a little hollow and looked curiously around at the man on his back.

Scott had put some sugar in his pocket that morning for the purpose of opening up friendly relations with his new mount and he promptly produced a lump. The horse accepted it after an inquisitive sniff and the battle was over. He did not seem to be at all distressed by the terrific race he had run and nibbled a little willow bush apparently at perfect ease. He seemed perfectly reconciled to his new partnership.

The next thing was to get him home. He had been bridle broken in a way. That is, he had been led around a little, but he had never been driven and knew nothing of a rider's management. He pricked up his ears and arched his neck when Scott gently gathered up the reins and spoke to him calmly, but he knew nothing of the "clucks" which usually urge a horse ahead, and Scott was afraid to slap him or nudge him with his heels. He pulled on one rein and succeeded in turning him toward home, but that was all.

Suddenly the great horse raised his beautiful head and with ears pricked forward gazed intently at the rim of the rise of ground ahead of him. His keen ears had caught the thud of pounding hoofs from the direction of the town. Scott could not hear them, but he guessed what had attracted the horse's attention. He waited expectantly for he did not know what effect the approach of other horses would have on his high-strung mount.

A moment later a bunch of hard riding horsemen swept over the crest of the knoll. At the sight of Scott sitting calmly erect on his fingernail saddle they stopped in astonishment and then sent forth a mighty shout of admiration, the tribute of expert horsemen to the nerve of a man who had dared what few of them would have done. They realized perfectly the danger of rushing down on this newly tamed horse and rode slowly and quietly down the slope.

The cautious approach seemed to arouse the suspicion of the big black. He advanced a few steps toward them proudly. He was a leader and in no mind to be trapped as he had often seen those same riders trap less wary animals. With a defiant toss of his lordly head he broke into a graceful trot and circled swiftly to the left. Beyond the last rider he struck a swinging gallop and headed for town. The cowboys' horses were pretty well blown with the long race and did not care to push the homeward pace. So the great stallion, none the worse for his wild dash for liberty, proudly and with many a backward glance, led the procession back down the main street of the town.

The people came to the doors and gazed in awe at this mysterious stranger who had tamed Jed Clark's wildest outlaw; and with such a saddle. Scott was beginning to wonder where the horse would take him and how he would ever get off, when the supervisor rode suddenly out of the alley ahead of him. At the sight of the other horse the black stopped for an instant, and Scott took advantage of the opportunity to dismount.

The supervisor jumped from his horse and hurried to meet him. "By George," he exclaimed, grasping Scott's hand, "I'm glad to see you. I was just starting out to look for your remains. You must be some rider."

"No," Scott laughed, "but I had some ride. I was just wondering how I would ever get off when you rescued me."

The big horse was used to being led by his bridle and stood quietly enough.

Mr. McGoorty ran up puffing and grabbed Scott's hand away from Mr. Ramsey. "Begorra, young man, I'm proud to shake your hand. You can come from Massachusetts or Peru or any place you please, now, and the boys will have nothing to say about it. Here, let me put that horse in my stable."

Scott caressed the big black and gave him another lump of sugar before he let McGoorty lead him away.

"Yes," said Mr. Ramsey, "you've made good with the boys all right. Here they come now and you'll find them different."

And they were. It was half an hour before Mr. Ramsey could tear Scott away from them and get him up to the office.

CHAPTER III
SCOTT FINDS A NEW HOME

When Scott came over to the hotel for his noon meal he found things very much changed. There was none of the sneering contempt which had so maddened him in the morning. His conquest of the big black had gained for him the admiration of the cowboys. They were all very friendly, so friendly in fact, that it was rather embarrassing, for their friendliness nearly always took the form of an invitation to drink which Scott courteously but firmly refused to do. The boys could not understand this very well, but they were willing to respect the rights of a man who could ride a wild horse with a fingernail saddle, and they soon ceased to bother him.

Soon after lunch the supervisor came in hurriedly. "Burton," he said, "I find that I shall not be able to go out with you in the morning, so I shall have to go this afternoon if you can get ready."

"Sure," Scott replied, "the sooner the better. I am ready to start any time."

"You can take your blankets along now, and I'll send your duffle up with the next pack train. You get your blankets and I'll get out your horse. Mine is out in front now."

Scott hurried upstairs to get his blanket roll. As he had told Mr. Ramsey he was ready to go with him, but he was wondering to himself whether he could do it. If the big horse happened to want to go in that direction all would be well, but if he did not Scott felt that he would probably go somewhere else. He was a little afraid that his second ride might not end as fortunately as his first, but he put on a bold face and carried the blanket roll to the stable as confidently as he could.

Mr. Ramsey had led out the black and was looking him over. Mr. McGoorty had followed Scott out.

"Do you really want to use that English saddle?" the supervisor asked.

"No," Scott answered, "It is the only kind I have ever used but it would make me too conspicuous, and I might as well get used to a stock saddle now. It must be better or every one here would not use it."

"You'll find it a lot more convenient," said the supervisor, evidently relieved. "A fellow nearly always has a bunch of duffle to carry along and there is no place to put it on that fingernail affair. One of these stock saddles is nearly as good as a trunk for packing stuff."

"Take one of mine and try it out," said McGoorty. He had taken a great fancy to Scott and was very solicitous to see that he did nothing to spoil the reputation he had so well started.

Scott took pains to make friends with the horse which seemed to remember him, submitted to his caresses and nuzzled the side of his coat for the expected lump of sugar. With McGoorty's help Scott managed to get the ponderous stock saddle in place and the strange cinches properly fastened. It was not done without a struggle for the big fellow was not at all sure that he liked it, but kindness seemed to have a great influence over him, and a little petting did more to soothe him than twenty men.

Mr. Ramsey backed off to look at him. "Gee, he certainly is a beauty," he exclaimed admiringly. "Will you let me try him this afternoon?"

Scott hesitated. "The boys might think that I was afraid to ride him again," he said doubtfully.

"Don't let that worry you," McGoorty said, "you showed your nerve this morning and can do what you please now."

"Then you better ride him," Scott said, "it was only luck this morning that he did not break my neck. I had no control over him and could not make him go anywhere that he did not want to go. If we want to go anywhere in particular this afternoon you better take him. But," he added decidedly, "if there is any question of making good I'll ride him if he kills me."

"All right," laughed the supervisor, "he will get plenty of chance to do that later. You tie that blanket roll back of my saddle and take my horse." Mr. Ramsey was an expert horseman and really wanted to give the horse a little training. He was pleased at Scott's attitude. He led the big black out into the street and waited for Scott to mount. McGoorty whispered to him furtively, "Jed is crazy because the kid got that stallion away from him. He is going to get even with the kid if he can. You better warn him."

Mr. Ramsey nodded. "All ready?" he called to Scott.

Scott answered by swinging the hanging rein over the horse's head and scrambling into the saddle. He made a rather undignified mount because he had not counted on the Western pony's habit of starting forward as soon as the rein is in place. It is up to the rider to catch the stirrup at once; his failure to do so makes the horse nervous. However, Scott managed to crawl on even though he missed the stirrup. Mr. Ramsey mounted at the same time, prepared for trouble. The black seemed a little startled at first and reared almost straight up, but a gentle voice reassured him and he quieted down.

"Ride ahead a little," Mr. Ramsey called, "and he'll come along. He does not know much about being driven."

Scott trotted his mount down the street and the black quickly overtook him. He could not bear to have another horse ahead of him.

For a few miles they rode in silence while Mr. Ramsey worked patiently to get the black very gradually accustomed to control. He found him much more amenable to the tone of the voice than he was to the bit. He could talk him into almost anything.

"Burton," Mr. Ramsey called enthusiastically as they turned into a little side valley which led back into the mountains, "I believe you have the best horse in the Southwest. There does not seem to be anything mean about him. Go slow with him, talk to him gently, keep your temper, and you'll never have any trouble with him. Go easy on the bit, remember that he does not know anything and will learn slowly, and he'll be trained before you know it. What are you going to name him?"

"I have been thinking about that," Scott replied, "and I think I shall call him 'Jed.'"

Mr. Ramsey made a wry face and then laughed, "Sort of hard on the horse, but good enough for Jed. By the way, Jed is pretty sore at losing him and will try very hard to get even with you."

"I thought I was just getting even with him," Scott said. "He expected to break my neck and he almost succeeded."

"That is true enough, but it is not the way that Jed looks at it. He is a mean customer and I advise you not to get mixed up with him. He's quick on the draw and the surest shot in the country. He has caused trouble for every patrolman we have ever had on this district."

"What should I expect from him?" Scott asked seriously.

"Everything, but of course his chief object will be to run in about twice as many sheep as he is paying for. Heth will be assigned to you as an extra guard. He knows the sheep business from A to Z and can put you onto all their tricks."

They rode out of the little cañon to a high bench on the mountain side. There was a large open plain on the bench, known as a "park," and beyond it the thinly timbered slopes led up to the higher ridges. The cañon up which they had come looked like a slit in the ground, and on either side of it the level plain stretched out toward the main valley where it fell abruptly to the valley level in an almost perpendicular cliff.

"The boundary of this forest," the supervisor explained, "follows the edge of that cliff for about five miles. This cañon is the most important approach from the valley, the only one in fact that the stockmen can use. That fence and gateway there is the chute and the sheep are counted as they come in."

They crossed the park and followed a winding, sidehill trail up across the face of the slope. The stand of trees was so open and there was so little underbrush that it did not seem to Scott much like the Northern forests he had known.

"That big locked box there," Mr. Ramsey explained again, "is a tool cache. It is filled with fire-fighting tools. The ranger will furnish you with a pass key and give you all the necessary instructions."

They came to the fork in the trail. "That one to the left," said Mr. Ramsey, "leads over to your headquarters, but we'll go on to the ranger cabin and he'll bring you back here."

Some three miles farther on and over the ridge lay the ranger's headquarters. Scott paused on the ridge and looked back. It was unlike anything he had ever seen. The wonderfully clear atmosphere made everything stand out with equal intensity whether it was one or twenty miles away. The size of the object alone gave one an idea of the distance; if there was no known object in sight for comparison the distance remained unknown. The park they had left an hour before seemed right at their feet; the houses in the town far down in the valley looked like toys, but every detail of them was distinct.

The colors also seemed most unreal. There were no gray rocks and brown hillsides such as Scott had seen so often at home. The cliffs all took on various purple hues and what should have been a dull, dead brown had here a rich, attractive, reddish tinge. The shadows on the forested hillsides were the deepest purple.

"Think an artist was crazy if he painted those colors," Mr. Ramsey suggested, reading his thoughts.

"Have thought so more than once," Scott said. "Sort of makes up for the bareness, doesn't it?"

"Yes, I suppose it does look pretty bare to you coming straight from New England, but you'll learn to like it. It's not as bad as it looks."

On the other side of the ridge was a very similar view, except that the valley was not so deep and there was no town at the bottom. In the immediate foreground was a neat little cabin set back against the hill in a flower-spangled yard. The Stars and Stripes streaming from the flag pole proclaimed its official character. It was the quarters of Ranger Dawson, Scott's immediate boss.

They dropped down the trail to the cabin and Dawson came out to meet them. He was a local man who had been selected for his knowledge of the stock business and he had a very good record in the service. Somehow, Scott did not like the cold appraising look that the ranger gave him, but the welcome he received was cordial enough to satisfy any one. They dismounted at the gate.

"Mr. Dawson," said Mr. Ramsey, "this is your new patrolman, Scott Burton."

"Very glad to meet you," said Mr. Dawson warmly, but he could not waste much attention on a new patrolman when he had sighted the supervisor's new horse. "How in thunder did you get that horse, John?" he asked curiously.

"Burton bought him from Jed Clark this morning and I borrowed him this afternoon. Isn't he a dandy?"

"Didn't suppose Jed would sell him at any price," said Dawson looking enviously at the big black, "and I did not suppose that any one could ride him if he did."

"No one else supposed so either 'til Burton rode him this morning with a fingernail saddle. Jed was pretty sore because he did not break his neck and you'll have to keep an eye out to see that he does not slip anything over on Burton to get even."

Dawson looked Scott over again with increased interest and it seemed to Scott that his expression was harder than ever.

"You must be some rider," Dawson finally remarked.

"Get your horse, Dawson," Mr. Ramsey interrupted, "and we'll take Burton down to his new quarters."

They took a trail back along the ridge and soon dropped down into the head of a cañon on the slope opposite the ranger cabin, to the shack which was to be Scott's home through some of the most eventful months of his life. It was a rough board building with battened cracks, plain but neat. It contained only two bunks, a table, two chairs and a cook stove, but it commanded a beautiful view of the lower slopes and the valley beyond. It was just such a place as Scott had often pictured as an ideal camp.

"I told Heth to be here by three," said Dawson, looking impatiently at his watch. It was four-thirty.

While Scott was still absorbed in the view there was a scrambling sound in the cañon trail and a horseman came bobbing up, followed at some distance by a patient pack horse. The new arrival greeted Mr. Dawson and Mr. Ramsey rather casually and hardly nodded to Scott. He was evidently more interested in the black horse than in any of the men.

He was not a prepossessing looking man. Rather small and very dirty, with a decidedly peaked face and a shifting eye; he gave Scott the impression of a weazel. Whenever you looked at Heth he was looking some place else, but whenever you looked in another direction you felt that he was staring at you. He did not say anything about the horse and yet Scott felt sure that he knew all about it. On the whole he did not look like a very congenial companion with whom to share a twelve by sixteen cabin on a lonely mountain.

Dawson, who had been watching Scott sharply, seemed to guess his thoughts. "Heth will be stationed here with you as a guard," he explained. "You probably will not like him much at first, but he is a good fellow; he knows all about sheep and you will find him a big help."

Mr. Ramsey turned Jed into the corral and took over his own horse. "Well," he said, "I must be going down. Thanks for the ride, Burton. You have a wonderful horse there. Watch Jed Clark and don't let him slip anything over on you. So long and luck to you."

"Call me up in the morning and I'll give you your instructions," said Dawson and he disappeared down the cañon trail after the supervisor, leaving Scott standing near the door of the shack with the blanket roll still lying at his feet.

CHAPTER IV
SOMETHING ABOUT A HORSE THIEF

Scott stood gazing dreamily down the cañon trail 'til the sound of the horses' hoofs had died away in the distance. He was thinking that two men had escorted him up there to his shack, a duty which they had apparently considered very important, and had left him without any instructions and wholly dependent upon a subordinate. He had not yet learned that it is usually up to a man to work up his own job, but he was learning.

"Well," he thought, "maybe I should have asked them about the details of this work while I had the chance, but hanged if I ever let that rat-faced guard find out that I do not know anything."

He had taken an instinctive dislike to his guard, the dislike of a straightforward man to the shifty-eyed.

He was aroused from his reverie by the approach of the guard who had been watching him furtively from a clump of bushes at the edge of the corral. Scott watched him shuffle up the slope in listless fashion, and did not like his walk any better than his eyes.

"Homesick?" Heth asked in an insinuating tone.

"Not so you could notice it," Scott answered contemptuously, and from that moment they cordially hated each other. It was a fine beginning.

Scott picked out the bed which he thought Heth wanted and made it up for himself. He saw Heth set out the coffee for supper so he decided that he would have tea. He knew that it was a petty way to do things, but he felt that he had to do something to keep the guard from walking all over him.

He managed to avoid an open fight only by eating in comparative silence and putting in the evening writing a letter in which he vented his feelings by describing the guard in no complimentary terms. If he had known that the guard had arisen before he was awake and had read the letter he would not have wondered at the gentleman's bad humor at the breakfast table.

Scott was feeling a little more cheerful himself, after a good night's sleep and a long look at the view from the cabin door. He was inclined to be friendly, but his advances met with small success.

After breakfast he called up the ranger. Dawson was much more voluble over the 'phone than he had been in person the day before. If Scott had mourned the lack of instructions the evening before he was getting them now. It seemed to him as though Mr. Dawson was outlining his whole summer's work. He was to inspect all the trails and telephone lines in his district, inventory all the fire tool caches and make a report on materials needed. Heth was to examine the range to see if it was ready for the sheep and make a trip to town for some material needed for the counting chute.

It was something to do and he was anxious to get at it. Moreover, he wanted to get out and study his district so that he would not be altogether dependent upon his guard. He relayed the ranger's orders to the guard and started for the corral to look up Jed.

"Are you going with me?" Heth called.

"No," Scott replied, "I'm going out to look over the trails and telephone lines."

Jed was feeling pretty frisky in the cool of the morning and was not at all sure that he wanted to be caught, but the kind words fascinated him once more and he finally permitted Scott to caress him and bridle him without a struggle. Scott was about to throw on the saddle blanket when his hand struck something sharp. He examined it and found a large burr. Scott whistled. "We would have had a fine time, old boy, if I had put that under the saddle." He examined the whole blanket carefully but did not find anything more.

Heth was saddling his own horse and getting ready for the trip to town. He watched Scott mount and ride out of the corral. Scott thought that he showed extraordinary interest in him, but laid it to his horse and Heth's natural curiosity to see how he sat his horse.

"What time do you think you'll be back?" Scott called.

"Five or six," Heth replied indifferently.

"So shall I," Scott said, and rode slowly up to the ridge trail. Jed did not like traveling alone as well as he liked to go with another horse, but Mr. Ramsey had taught him a great deal in the short time he had ridden him and Scott had no trouble in managing him. He turned to the left on the ridge trail, the opposite direction to the way they had come in the day before, and proceeded to follow out the trails of his district by means of a small map.

It never occurred to Scott to look back and even if he had he probably would not have seen Heth who was standing in the bunch of brush beside the ridge trail watching him out of sight. No sooner was Heth sure of the course that Scott was taking than he hurried down to the cabin and grabbed the telephone. He took down the receiver very gently and listened. It was a party line and he wanted to be very sure that no one else was using it. Convinced that the line was clear he rang one short sharp ring, followed at a long interval by another. The call was not on the list and it very closely resembled the jingles so often produced by thunder storms in the mountains.

He listened patiently. A receiver clicked somewhere and a doubtful voice called "hello," but Heth did not answer, nor did he repeat his ring. After at least two minutes of silence a voice said, "Well."

"I'm going to town for chuck and chute stuff. He went south on trail and 'phone patrol. Burred his saddle this morning but he found it. Better get in rest of extras. Chute to-morrow. Cottonwood; eleven." He hung up the receiver, glanced at his watch and strolled out to his horse.

Far down the valley Jed Clark called his foreman and gave some orders to his herders. And Dawson, far up in his little mountain cabin, prepared to ride north.

Scott rode slowly on his way, serenely unmindful of all this, and enjoying life immensely. The thin, open stand of timber on these grassy lands with the apparent absence of animal life was entirely new to him. At every turn of the trail a new vista of vast extent and strange crystal clearness opened up before him. He could have spent hours in studying the beauties of the scenery if he had not been impelled by his desire to cover his district and get away from his dependence on his guard. As it was he saw what he could on the fly and picked out many a place to spend a Sunday afternoon later on.

The ranger had given him to understand that he would probably find the trails and telephone lines in pretty bad shape, but so far he had found them both in almost perfect condition. He began to think that Heth must be a good guard, no matter how disagreeable he might be personally. Noon found him on a high grassy bench on the extreme southern edge of his district. Miles of mountain and valley spread out before him in almost boundless panorama, and it appealed to him as an ideal place for lunch.

He did not know exactly what to do with Jed. Western horses are not used to being tied and he was afraid that Jed was not well enough trained to stand without it. However, he had to make a beginning with him sometime and he decided to try him. Jed seemed to know what was expected of him. He grazed contentedly on a small area, and showed no tendency to wander off.

The sun was very warm and Scott went back to the shade of a tree to eat his lunch and enjoy the scenery. Before he was half through lunch he was glad to crawl out into the sun again to get warm. He was soon to learn that no matter how hot the sun might be in that high altitude it was seldom warm enough in the shade for comfort.

He had finished his lunch and was lolling lazily in the sunshine when he discovered a new animal, the first he had seen in the country. He did not know what it was at first. Its movements resembled those of a squirrel, but its head seemed abnormally large. He sneaked up on it and discovered the secret. It was a squirrel but it was carrying a large pine cone by the end. It was a beautiful creature with tasseled ears like a lynx. It was somewhat smaller than the Eastern gray squirrel and instead of a rusty, sandy color its coat was a clear Maltese gray and the whole under side of him was a sparkling white. Scott had always been interested in all the wild animals and birds, and he had followed this new squirrel quite a ways back into the woods to get a good look at him and observe something of his habits.

The sudden whinnying of horses on the bench startled him and he ran back to the edge of the woods to learn what had happened. There in the open was a strange horseman cautiously approaching Jed with whirling lariat. Scott's first impulse was to shout his protest, but he changed his mind and standing in the edge of the woods awaited silently to see the outcome.

Jed stood like a statue with tail arched and head erect watching the whirling rope. He looked like an easy mark. The rider was very slowly getting within roping distance. Suddenly the rope shot out like a long arm and the widespread loop hung directly over Jed's head. It looked like a sure catch, but Jed had dodged that flying rope too often to be caught so easily. He ducked with the grace of a dancer and trotting a little to one side awaited the next throw. The horseman swore volubly and coiled his rope doggedly for another try. Three times he threw and failed. Jed's maneuvering had brought him around nearer to the forest and the rider caught sight of Scott standing in the shadow of the trees. He misinterpreted Scott's silence and rode toward him, coiling his rope as he came.

"What 'ell you give me to catch him for you, sonny?" he asked with a patronizing sneer.

Scott's blood boiled, but he remembered Mr. Ramsey's caution and tried to keep his temper in spite of the insult. "Do you get many that way?" he asked coldly.

"What way?" the cowboy asked, surprised at this tone coming from a man whom he supposed to be too scared to talk.

"Saddle horses," Scott replied tersely.

"Look a here, young feller, there's been many a man buried here for less than that," the cowboy blustered, laying his hand threateningly on his revolver.

"Yes," Scott replied, "and there's been many a one hung for roping other people's horses."

The cowboy glared at Scott with malignant ferocity. He was no coward and seeing that Scott was unarmed had started to dismount when he suddenly remembered why Jed Clark had sent him into the mountains that morning. His manner changed suddenly.

"Well, bo," he chuckled, "you've got the right stuff in you all right. Can't bluff you, can they? Most of them Eastern fellers I've seen out here would run if a man so much as looked at his gun. I was just tryin' you out."

Scott looked at him in silence, not deigning to answer. He was not at all misled by his sudden change of front and he longed to tell him so, but he wanted to see what the man was really after.

"You're the new patrolman, ain't you?" the cowboy continued genially in spite of the frost.

"You ought to know," Scott replied cuttingly, "I saw you at the corral with Jed Clark when I bought this horse."

"You bet I was," said the cowboy not in the least disconcerted, "and a blamed good job you made of it. That's the best horse in the Southwest if you could ride him. Jed's changed his mind about him now and he's sorry he sold him."

"You're mistaken about his changing his mind," Scott retorted, "he never intended to sell him."

Jed had chosen his man well. He ignored the rebuff and maintained a genial countenance. "When I seen him standing out there this morning all saddled I thought maybe he had throwed you back there on the trail som'eres—liable to throw anybody, that horse is—and I was thinking to rope him and take him up to the cabin for you."

It was such a plausible story that Scott wavered for a moment, but he remembered the ugly looks the cowboy had given him when he opened the conversation, and contented himself with a dry, "Thanks."

"Looking over your grazing land?" the cowboy continued by way of casual conversation.

"Yes," Scott replied shortly.

"Lucky for you fellers that the range will always support about twice as many as the government estimates."

"Will they?" Scott asked innocently. He was interested about anything he could learn of the grazing industry.

"Sure they will. How could you feed them extras if they didn't?"

"There will not be any extras on here," Scott answered firmly.

"No?" said the cowboy inquiringly. "It's pretty easy money," he insinuated.

"Did you come up here to bribe me?" Scott asked indignantly.

"Bribe you?" exclaimed the cowboy in injured surprise. "Who, me? Gosh, no. I don't own no sheep. Never liked the smellin' critters. But there's lots of places where the sheep men do work in thousands of head that way and the patrolmen make good money on it."

"And cheat the government that hires them," Scott exclaimed hotly.

The cowboy had turned his head to hide a smile. "There's a lot of people around this country that considers cheating the government a pretty good part of their business, and the best payin' part."

"That business," said Scott with determination as he strode over to where Jed was feeding near them and mounted him, "is just what I have come out here to stop, and you can tell Jed Clark so when you get back."

"Of course it ain't none of my business," said the cowboy indifferently, "but Jed will have extras on here one way or another and if I was you I'd rather make something out of it than lose my job for it."

"Maybe I am not going to do either," Scott said quietly, and with the faintest trace of a bow he rode away on his trail patrol.

"Fool," muttered the cowboy as he watched Scott out of sight. "He has plenty of nerve, but Jed will get his goat. Then maybe Heth will go in and we will have peace for a while."

CHAPTER V
A DAY WITH THE SMALL RANCHERS

Scott was awakened the next morning by the rattle of dishes and found that Heth had breakfast all ready to go on the table. Whatever other shortcomings might be attributed to the guard he could hardly be called lazy. He never objected to any job that was assigned to him, was continually busy when around the camp, was up early and came in late. Scott recognized all this and realized the perfect knowledge that the man seemed to have of every phase of the forest work. He bounded out of bed thoroughly ashamed of himself.

"Why didn't you call me?" Scott exclaimed.

Heth seemed somewhat surprised at the irritated tone. "Breakfast wasn't ready," he replied simply.

"I did not mean it that way," Scott replied, a little taken back, "but I want to do my share of the work around here. I intended to help you get breakfast, but the high altitude seems to make me sleep like a hammer."

"Gets them all that way when they first come up," Heth replied pleasantly. "Might as well sleep it out. I wake up anyway and don't mind getting breakfast. I'm used to it."

Heth's pleasant manner was so different from his grouch of the morning before that Scott felt even more ashamed of himself and wondered if he had misjudged the man. "Well, I'll try to make up for it later," he sputtered through the cold spring water, and as he dried the few breakfast dishes he felt happier than he had at any time since he first met Heth.

"How does the big black go?" Heth asked. "Have any trouble with him?"

"No," Scott replied, warming up on the subject of his horse, "he behaved splendidly; but I had a funny experience yesterday." And he explained in detail how the strange horseman had attempted to steal Jed. He kept quiet about the rest of the conversation.

Heth listened excitedly and did not let on that he had seen the horseman afterward and heard his version of the story. "Maybe he was trying to catch him for you," Heth said. "No one ever thought that anybody could ride that horse and they all expect him to kill you before you have had him very long."

"It's possible," Scott said doubtfully, "but I don't believe it. He was with Jed Clark the day I bought the horse, and I know Jed had no idea of selling him."

Heth had his own reasons for not pushing the matter and a ring at the 'phone interrupted any further talk on the subject.

It was the ranger. He ordered Scott to find how much stock the ranchers would have for free use and have Heth fix up the chute ready for the counting of the sheep. Scott again relayed the orders to Heth.

"I suppose you know all about this business, but it is pretty much Greek to me. How do you find out about the free use stock?" The day before Scott would never have asked Heth this question, but this morning he felt more friendly, and he knew it was the sensible thing to do.

"Nothing to it," Heth replied, "except a long ride. Just go to see each one, ask him how many head he is going to run on the forest this year and give him a permit if he is under the limit. There are some forms here for it."

Heth produced the forms and Scott looked them over carefully.

"Looks simple enough. If he has too many I suppose I give him a permit for the limit and charge him for the rest."

"No, you give him a permit for the limit and report the overrun to the ranger. He attends to that."

"Is there a list of these settlers?" Scott asked.

"No, but I can tell you who they all are and they live in a string in the valley along the edge of the forest. The ones farther out are the big fellows and we do not have to monkey with them. They get theirs at the super's office."

With this information in hand Scott saddled up Jed, who was getting very much attached to his kind master, and started down the trail to the valley. Heth rode with him as far as the sheep chute, and pointed out the sheep trails he had posted with new signs the day before. "You see," he explained, "you can't let them wander all over or they would never get where they were going. They would be grazing on somebody else's range all summer. So we post these trails which they have to follow and we limit the time they can have to get to their own range. Each man has a range allotted to him and has to stay on it."

"Do they all come in at the same time?" Scott asked. He wanted to get all the information he could on it before he came in contact with the ranchers themselves. Heth already knew he was green but he did not want the ranchers to find it out.

"Don't have to," Heth replied, "but they will this year. The winter range is just about played out and they will want to get into the hills as soon as possible. That means that the whole bunch of them will be crowding in to-morrow. You will probably meet some of them on their way up to-day."

Scott stopped for a few minutes to examine the chute. It was made of two fences which were built to form an hour glass. The sheep were driven into the broad funnel-shaped entrance which narrowed down till there was room for only one or two sheep to go through at a time.

"You sit up there," Heth explained, "and count them as they go through. It's some job when they get to crowding and piling up, but easy enough most of the time."

"Is there any way to stop them if they get to coming too fast?" Scott asked.

"Couldn't stop them with a four bar gate after the leader has gone through. You can keep pretty good track of them after you get used to it. We had one fellow here who used to be a whirlwind at counting before the chute was built. They could not come too fast for him. Some guy asked him how he did it. 'Easy enough,' he says, 'count their feet and divide by four.'"

"Well," Scott laughed, "I guess I can manage it all right then if they all have the same number of feet. See you at supper." He rode on down the steep trail alone. He felt that now for the first time he was really doing a patrolman's work. Yesterday's ride was designed to acquaint him with the trails, but to-day he was doing something which would go on record. Just how much of a record he was going to make that day he did not dream at the time.

Once out of the cañon Jed struck a long, swinging pace which made the valley slip by like a panorama, and soon brought him to the home of the first small rancher. The man was just about to mount his horse when Scott rode up. He returned a sullen nod to Scott's cheery greeting.

"Mr. Simpson?" Scott asked, pausing in the act of dismounting. He was feeling particularly friendly himself this morning and the other's cold manner grated on him. "More Western hospitality," he thought.

"You guessed it," Mr. Simpson answered briefly.

"I am the patrolman for district three of the National Forest," Scott explained. The man knew perfectly well who he was and Scott knew that he knew, but an introduction seemed necessary to crack the ice. The man made no answer.

"I want to find out," Scott continued, anxious to get through with this old grouch as soon as possible, "how many head of stock you want to run on the forest this year on your free use permit?"

"How much is this 'free use' going to cost this year," the man asked sarcastically.

"Cost?" Scott exclaimed in surprise.

"I think that is what I said," the man drawled, "Cost."

"First time I ever heard of a free use permit costing anything," Scott retorted. The man's ugly manner and a feeling that he was being guyed angered Scott.

"Cost me a dollar a head, last year," the man persisted with an ugly sneer.

"How did that happen?" Scott asked a little doubtfully. He was almost sure that he would get a "joshing" answer of some kind to this question and he did not feel in the humor to take it.

"'Cause that's what that robber patrolman demanded," the man exploded. "Think I offered it to him voluntarily?"

"I don't see why you should pay a patrolman for a free use permit either voluntarily or any other way," Scott retorted.

"Hicks over here on the next ranch could not see it either," Simpson replied, "and all his sheep died of the loco weed."

"Do you mean to say that the patrolman poisoned them?" Scott exclaimed in horror.

"I'd say he did," the man answered fiercely.

"Why didn't you report him to the ranger?" Scott asked.

"Lot of good that would do and he knew it," the man growled.

Scott was perplexed. He did not like to listen to the slander of his service and yet if it was true it ought to be investigated. He wisely decided to end the discussion now and investigate it later.

"Well, Mr. Simpson," he said with dignity, "possibly this has been done in the past, and possibly that is the reason that the man was fired. I don't know anything about it and I did not come here to hear the service accused of graft. I came to find out how many head of stock you wanted on free use permit and I am not used to being accused of graft. If you do not want a permit, say so."

Simpson eyed him for a moment in silence and then said briefly, "Put me down for the limit."

"Any extras?" Scott asked as he made out the permit.

"Thought the ranger took care of that." Simpson objected suspiciously.

"So he does," Scott replied, "but I am supposed to report where there are any."

"All right," Simpson said, "tell him I'll have a hundred."

"If the sheep on that permit cost you anything, let me know," Scott said a little pompously, as he handed over the permit.

"Going to Hicks' place?" Simpson asked in a suddenly friendly tone as he put the permit in his pocket.

Scott nodded.

"I'll ride over with you," Simpson volunteered.

Scott was somewhat surprised at the sudden change of manner, but gladly accepted the offer. Simpson soon won his way into Scott's good graces by his generous praises of Jed and before they had covered the two miles to Hicks' place they were on very good terms.

Mr. Hicks had ridden out to look over his stock but they soon found him. He was a jolly little Irishman with sparkling blue eyes which danced when he recognized the new patrolman. "Howdy," he responded to Scott's greeting, "I see you are still sticking to that horse."

"You bet," Scott replied enthusiastically, "I've never had a better one." He did not explain that he had never had another one. "I came over to see how many head of stock you are going to put on your free use permit this spring."

Hicks winked at Simpson. "Out collecting his fees before he fair knows the way home," he chuckled. "Well, how much do I have to pay this year to keep my sheep out of that loco patch?"

His manner was friendly enough but Scott thought he recognized a certain shrewd hardness back of it and when he remembered what Simpson had told him he did not blame him. "I've been through all that with Mr. Simpson," Scott replied a little haughtily, "and I don't care to hear it again. I am new here and I know nothing of what happened last year and I will not be accused of graft. A free use permit means free use to me. If you want one I am here to give it to you; if you don't want it I have a long way to ride."

"Give me the limit, me boy, and shake hands on it."

Scott gladly shook hands. He liked this little Irishman. "Any extras?" he asked and he felt the little man start perceptibly.

"So that's where you come in?" Hicks exclaimed.

"That's where I will come in if you insist," Scott replied hotly. "It is my duty to report to the ranger where there are any extras and I do not propose to be insulted every time I ask for the information."

"Tut, tut, no offense was meant. Tell Dawson I'll have fifty. If you knew what I know you would not be surprised. Besides it is what you are going to get wherever you go so you might as well get used to it."

"Then I shall probably lick somebody before night," Scott laughed.

"And I'm going along to help you," said Hicks pocketing his permit.

So they all three rode down the valley to Bradish's where Scott met with the same suspicious reception, made the same explanation and finally rode on down the valley with Mr. Bradish added to the little troop. He could not understand the readiness with which each man offered to accompany him, but his advance was like that of a snow ball. Each rancher he saw promptly took out a permit for free use and joined the procession.

When they reached Wren's place at noon there were six in the party. Mr. Wren, a big, rough, raw-boned fellow, was so blunt in his insinuations that Scott was furious before the permit was finally written, but Wren did not seem to notice it. With the permit safe in his pocket he looked the rest of the bunch over curiously. "Where is this crowd bound for? If it's any of my business," he asked.

"Up to Bronson's," was the prompt reply.

"Party there?" Wren asked. A party in this thinly settled country was a great event and every one who heard about it came regardless of distance or invitation.

"Guess there will be when we all get there," said Simpson with a grin.

"Come on in to dinner," said Wren turning toward the house, "and I'll ride over with you."

They all accepted the invitation as a matter of course, and Scott, still smarting from Wren's rough speeches, mounted Jed to continue his journey, wondering where he would find a meal. He had expected to get dinner at one of the ranches and had not counted on them being hostile to the Service.

Wren happened to turn just as he was settling into the saddle. "Hey," he shouted. Scott paused. "Where do you think you're going?"

Scott had not had a civil word from Wren since he arrived and was not in a humor to be ordered around now. "To Brown's," he answered shortly, and added, "If it's any of your business."

"Turning down my invitation to dinner are you?" he asked in an ominously gentle voice. To ignore an invitation to dinner was considered a deadly insult and the others all stared expectantly.

"I do not care to eat at a home where I am called a grafter and looked on with suspicion," Scott answered with dignity. He had sized his man up and felt pretty certain that he would get the worst of a fight but he was an experienced boxer and was not at all dismayed by the prospect.

Wren, who had been advancing toward Jed with mighty strides, stopped suddenly at this retort and looked at Scott silently for almost a minute. When he spoke his voice was gentle again but it was not the gentleness of intense anger this time. "Well, young man, this is the first time I ever had a man ignore my invitation to dinner and didn't try to kill him, but this time I reckon you're right. I reckon I would not eat with a man myself who talked that way to me, but if you had had the experiences that I have in the last five years you wouldn't hold it against me. I thought you were passing us up because we were not good enough for you. Some Easterners think that way. If I hadn't believed you honest, I wouldn't have asked you to dinner. If you'll come in we'll be glad to have you."

It was the longest speech that Wren had ever been known to make and his friends looked at him in admiration. Scott was only too glad to accept the apology and get out of his trouble so easily. He dismounted and extended his hand. "If that is the way you feel, Mr. Wren, I shall be delighted to come in," he said heartily.

Mrs. Wren, a large motherly woman, met them at the door. She was not at all dismayed by the unexpected dinner party and greeted them cordially. Visitors here were few and always welcome. "Mother," bawled Mr. Wren, once more restored to his boisterous self, "Here is an honest patrolman."

Such was Scott's introduction. It troubled him to hear the service spoken of in that way, but he knew that they did not mean it for an insult to him and tried to overlook it. The inside of the 'dobe house was as neat and clean as a pin and the ham and eggs were of the best. All in all they had a jolly time and Scott was certainly glad that he got in on it. He learned to know these people in that brief time as he could never have learned to know them in any other way.

After dinner the little cavalcade rode on to Brown's, to Mathey's and finally to Bronson's. The result everywhere was the same. Distrust, incredulity, acceptance and cordiality.

When Scott signed the last permit it was four o'clock in the afternoon and he was sixteen miles from home. "Sorry I can't stay to the party, gentlemen," he said pleasantly, "but I am a long way from home and I have to be out on that chute early in the morning counting sheep. The whole bunch will be rushing in on us to-morrow."

"Well, me boy," said little Mr. Hicks speaking for them all, "you won't be missing much, because you are the party. You have given us the first square deal we have had in several years and we came along to see you through. We'll ride back with you whenever you are ready to go, but I want to tell you while we are all here together that we appreciate this and we are going to back you up whenever you need it. And unless I miss my guess an honest man coming into that district is going to need backing."

Scott thanked them profusely. "Possibly some of you have had a raw deal from some individual," he exclaimed, "but the service intends to give every man a square deal, and I am going to try to see that you all get it."

They swept away up the valley like a crowd of care-free school-boys. Each shouted a friendly good-by as he dropped out at his home. When the last man had dropped out and Scott was riding on alone he felt as though he had left old friends. All along the cañon trail he passed by what seemed to him a countless ocean of sheep, tired out by their long day's drive and all bedded down for the night waiting for the chance to get onto the green mountain range in the morning. Their continuous bleating had a strange, weird sound to Scott's unaccustomed ears. It was late when he reached the cabin but he found Heth waiting supper for him.

In bed that night he thought over the strange experiences of the day. There was not another people in the world who would have done such a thing and he liked it. For some reason which he did not stop to analyze he had not told Heth anything about it.

CHAPTER VI
A FOREST FIRE

Scott was up before day the next morning and he and Heth prepared a hurried breakfast. He was quite excited. He had read volumes about the myriad sheep which were grazed in the national forests of the great Southwest and he was anxious to see them. The fact that he was now going to have an actual part in the handling of them made him impatient to get things going.

Heth had everything ready at the chute for counting in the sheep and Scott had all the permits in hand approved by the supervisor, stating just how many sheep each owner had paid for. Of course each herder knew just how many he was supposed to take in and just what range had been allotted to him. It was Scott's job to count the sheep as they came through the chute and see that the permits were not exceeded. As the old gentleman had told Scott on the train, the arrangement was comparatively new and many of the stockmen were by no means reconciled to the forest service control. They had been running their stock free on those ranges for years and they were not going to pay for the privilege without a struggle. It was almost certain that there would be more than one attempt to exceed the limit. Mr. Ramsey had told him as much and he was anxious for the test.

At last the breakfast things were cleared away and they were ready for the start. Scott caught up a little tally register such as the headwaiters in a hotel dining room use, looked over the permits to see that he had them all and started for the corral. It was light now and time they were off.

Of course it was an old story to Heth and there was no reason why he should be excited about it, but it seemed to Scott that he was unnecessarily slow and apparently getting more nervous every minute. Just outside the cabin Heth mumbled an excuse about some forgotten article and went back. Scott, too impatient to wait for him any longer, went on down to saddle Jed.

Heth peeped out of the door to make sure that Scott was out of earshot and hurried to the telephone, but it rang before he got there. He snatched down the receiver and answered eagerly, and a look of relief came over his face when he recognized the ranger's voice. "Hello, Heth, is Burton there?"

"Just is," replied Heth a little irritably. "He's already gone down to saddle up. Hold the line and I'll call him."

Heth shouted from the cabin door and Scott hurried up from the corral exasperated at the further delay. "Dawson's on the line," Heth explained.

Scott took the receiver. "Yes? Good morning, Mr. Dawson.... Fire.... Hadn't I better send Heth over there, he knows the country better?"

Heth smiled and looked out of the window.

"Oh, very well, sir," Scott concluded in an aggrieved tone. "I can handle it. I'll report as soon as I get back."

He turned from the telephone keenly disappointed and found Heth looking at him inquiringly.

"Dawson says that the lookout has reported a fire over on the north edge of our district. He does not think that I know enough about sheep to handle the job here alone and wants me to leave that to you and go look up that hanged fire."

"Then I suppose I shall have to sit on that fence all day and count sheep while you take a little ride for your health," Heth growled with well-feigned disgust.

"I wish you had my job," Scott complained. "I've fought a good many fires, but I've never seen two thousand sheep in my life. Well, I'll hustle all I can and I may get back in time to see some of it."

Scott ran down to the corral again to finish saddling Jed and soon came clattering back to the cabin door. Heth was just coming out in a big hurry. All signs of dallying had disappeared. "Have you got that tally register?" he called.

Scott pulled it out of his pocket, Heth snatched it and started for his horse.

"How is the best way to get over there?" Scott called after him, "the Knobcone trail?"

"Yes," Heth called back without stopping, "Knobcone and turn to the left."

"If he'd been in half as much of a hurry a while ago," Scott growled, "we would have been gone before that 'phone message came."

He rode off doggedly along the ridge and turned off into the Knobcone trail. That was the only trail in the district of any length that he had not been over, but he had his map and did not anticipate any trouble in following it. Most of the trails had been well built, were in good condition and were plainly marked. The trail rose steadily and kept him from making as good time as he had hoped. Knobcone mountain towered high above him and three miles ahead when he came to an unmarked fork in the trail.

"Of course," Scott thought, "the only unmarked fork on the forest because I am in a hurry and do not know this country." He pulled out his map. No such fork appeared. He could see the trail he was on leading straight away up the steep slope to the peak and his first impulse was to follow it, for he was sure that he could see all the north country from there. But Heth had said to take the trail to the left. Possibly it circled the peak and would bring him out on the north side without the climb. In that case it would undoubtedly be quicker; and that decided him.

For a mile or so the trail promised well. It followed a contour line around the face of the hill and seemed to be leading just where Scott wanted to go. The country was open, with only a scattering stand of bull pine. The trail which followed a little natural bench had required very little building, but it was distinct and offered good traveling. Scott was making good time and having visions of counting some of the sheep in spite of the fire when Jed came to a sudden stop on the edge of a steep cañon.

The trail dived into it and was quickly lost in a dense growth of Engelmann's spruce. Some of the spruces poked so high up out of the cañon that he could not see the other side. The descent was so steep that he was afraid to try Jed on it till he found out where it came out. So he dismounted and scrambled down on foot. The trail was very narrow and the needles on the protruding spruce boughs stuck through his clothes like thorns. He had misgivings of ever being able to get Jed through there.

The cañon, instead of being a mere cut in the mountain side as he had expected, was flat bottomed and broad. The trail continued to thread its way through the spruce thicket, distinct but crooked. It seemed more like a foot trail than a horse trail, and Scott looked in vain for any hoof prints. He considered going across on foot to the north slope—it could not be much over a mile now—to where he could see the valley beyond. He would lose a great deal of time now if he attempted to ride back to the fork and up over the mountain peak. He hurried on, pricking his face and hands painfully on the spruce needles.

Suddenly he was confronted by a solid wall of spruce and a small sign reading "Th 7—'14." Scott gave an exclamation of disgust and started back over the trail at a run regardless of the spruce boughs which spurred him mercilessly at every jump. He knew what it was now. Some experimental plots for the study of the growth of spruce had been laid out there in the cañon and the trail was only a path leading to them. He stubbed his toe in his haste and dived head first into one of the prickly spruces.

"Heth may know all about sheep," he growled as he panted up the steep side of the cañon, "but he knows mighty little about the trails." And if he had had Heth right there then, he would probably have punched his head, for Jed was gone.

At first Scott thought that the horse had merely wandered a few steps in search of grass, but he could see quite a distance through the open woods and there was no sign of him. Certainly he would not have gone into that spruce thicket. He was involuntarily rubbing his hands and thighs as he looked about him and he could not imagine anything going into that hornet's nest if it did not have to.

Then he suddenly remembered the strange horseman who had tried to steal Jed a few days before. He hurriedly examined the place where he had left the horse and found holes plowed in the ground by plunging hoofs. Something had evidently startled him very suddenly for there was no sign that he had moved till he made the sudden lunge.

Scott tried to reason it out. If it was the horseman he must have come down the trail and if he had there would be tracks. He examined the back trail for some distance without finding any trace of another track of either horse or man. Adopting the tactics of an old hound that has lost the scent, he made a large circle, examining the ground carefully at every step, but he did not find anything till he came across Jed's tracks headed straight up the slope and still gouging the ground desperately at every jump. He completed his circle without finding any sign of anything having approached the horse.

Scott was badly puzzled but there was no time to figure it out now. He had already lost an hour and a half. The next thing was to find the horse. He took the running trail up the slope and followed it. At least it was going in the direction which he wanted to take. But even this advantage was only temporary for the tracks soon began to turn back toward camp. Scott would have given up the chase then and gone about his business on foot had he not noticed that the tracks seemed to indicate a more moderate pace. He was about ready to give it up when he saw something moving in a little clearing ahead and sighted Jed.

The horse was evidently much excited. His neck was arched and his head was high. He would stand for a few seconds intently watching Scott's approach. Then, with head held to one side to avoid the long, dragging reins he would trot nervously around a little circle before coming to gaze once more. Scott approached him cautiously but could not get his hand on him. Every time he reached for the bridle Jed would trot another little circle. A sudden move to grab him sent him galloping to the other side of the opening.

Then Scott remembered that in his impatience and lack of breath he had neglected to speak softly. Ever since that first day when Jed had surrendered to that soft, persuasive voice it had been the tone that appealed to him. One could talk him into almost anything but he did not yet know what it was to be forced or caught by craft. "What's the matter, boy?" Scott asked quietly as he approached him once more, and Jed lowered his muzzle to Scott's hand in apparent relief.

Scott mounted and rode eastward to intercept the Knobcone trail on the higher slope. Jed traveled all right but seemed exceedingly nervous and shied badly several times when they were going under a tree. Something had evidently scared him pretty badly and that something seemed to have been in a tree. They lost a little more time picking a way across two or three bad gullies, but finally came out on the Knobcone trail about a mile from the peak. There were no trees on this upper slope and Jed lost all his nervousness and pegged away at the steep grade like a good fellow.

As they reached the top Scott stretched his neck eagerly for a look into the valley and sank back into the saddle with an exclamation of disgust. It was a twin peak and the second one stood square in his path. The trail followed the saddle between the two peaks and ascended the second one about a mile away. Scott glanced at his watch. It was one o'clock. That blunder of Heth's in misdirecting him had cost him at least three good hours. With a word to Jed he loped rapidly across the gentle dip of the saddle and was soon on top of the second peak.

There was nothing to interfere with the view there. It was magnificent. He seemed to be on the top of the world. There were plenty of other mountains but they all seemed lower, and far to the southwest was the main valley extending for miles and clear as crystal all the way. There was none of that hazy effect to which he had always been accustomed at home. And over there somewhere within range of his vision, if he had only known how to locate it, was the mighty seven thousand foot cut of the Grand Cañon.

"My," he thought, "what a splendid place this would be for a look out."

Only then did he remember why he had come. The magnificence of the view had carried him away. "Can see everything in the world from here except a fire. Not the faintest trace of smoke in all this end of Arizona. There's the lookout on that peak over there to the northeast. If that jay over there has a glass, as he probably has, he can see me over here gawking around looking for his fool fire."

He dismounted and settled down beside a rock for a careful survey of the country. He felt sure that there was no fire, for a smoke in that atmosphere would stand out like an electric sign in a country town, but he wanted to be entirely certain of it. Anyway it was already too late to see much of the sheep counting and he might as well take advantage of the opportunity to study the country.

Scott had always been very much interested in geology and he had never had a better chance. He had read much about that Southwest country. He knew that it had once been a great plateau which had eroded tremendously, leaving the mountain ridges and mesa tops at or near the original level, and cutting the valleys away to the level plains. And here it was all spread out before him like an open book. He could look across rows of mountain ridges practically all the same height and scattered about the plains were great square-sided, flat-topped mesas, of equal height and capped with the same hard substance. And he tried to imagine those mesas and ridges crumbling away, as they undoubtedly were doing, but so slowly that it could not be noticed, and the whole very gradually returning to a vast flat plain.

It was a fascinating picture and Scott found it hard to concentrate on the search for a wisp of smoke in the existence of which he had no faith. At last the lengthening shadows on the plains beside the mesas warned him that it was time to start for home. Jed was peacefully cropping the thin grass on the bald knob of the mountain peak and was in no more hurry to go than his master. With one more glance at the beauty of it all and one more determined search for smoke Scott mounted and turned Jed's head toward home.

He rode slowly, enjoying the scenery and still dreaming of the mighty changes which had built that remarkable country and did not realize till he came into the shadow of the timber on the southeastern slope, that darkness would overtake him before he could reach the cabin. There was still another and better reason for him to stop dreaming. With the return to the timber Jed's nervousness returned also. He nearly spilled Scott more than once by shying suddenly and dashing under a clump of trees at full speed.

So close is the relationship of a man to his horse that he soon communicated his nervousness to his rider. Scott could not see anything, but he had an uncomfortable feeling that he was being followed. The feeling became so strong that he determined to stop and see if there really was anything there. Jed did not fancy stopping in the timber, but Scott finally managed to bring him to a prancing halt on the far edge of a little open park. He glanced back and felt sure that he saw something in the trail just within the shadow of the trees. But it did not advance.

"Pshaw," Scott grumbled, "I'll be shying at a bunch of brush myself after awhile."

He rode on, determined not to look back, but the temptation became too strong. He cast a glance over his shoulder and was sure that he saw a silent shadow cross a little opening in the woods not fifty yards back. He rode ahead slowly and stopping again on the far edge of another little opening wheeled suddenly about.

This time his maneuver was successful. A large mountain lion loped lithely out of the shadow into the open before he seemed to realize how close he was. Scott had read of these queer animals trailing people silently for miles with no apparent object, but he had never believed it. No sooner did the great cat see them not more than thirty yards away than he stopped in apparent embarrassment and gazed indifferently about the country, neither advancing or retreating. Scott saw all this in the fraction of a second and longed for a rifle, but it would not have done him any good if he had had a whole arsenal—for Jed saw the cougar almost as soon as Scott did and ended the interview with one wild snort and a still wilder plunge which almost shook Scott out of the saddle.

There was no reasoning with him now. Neither soft words nor hard-curbed bit had any influence at all. By chance he happened to hit the trail—or so it seemed to Scott—and down it he went at a terrific pace. He paid no attention to grades or washouts, up hill or down, over smooth trail and broken ruts, he jumped four feet in the air over every shadow and seemed to duck under every tree. Scott leaned over on his neck to avoid the limbs and brush and clung on for dear life. That first ride over the corral fence and across the open plain was nothing to this. But Jed was as sure footed as a mountain goat. He swung out of the Knobcone trail safely and swept along the ridge with a burst of speed which was almost unbelievable.

Scott was wondering whether he would attempt to turn him down the trail to the cabin or let him run it out along the ridge, but he really did not have anything to say about it. Jed was in complete control of the home trip. He whirled into the side trail with a scattering of gravel and a suddenness that left Scott hanging to the saddle bow to avoid the bushes beside the trail, and stopped with all four feet sliding before the gate of the corral. He was trembling violently and when Scott came to dismount he found that he himself was trembling even worse. He tried to lead Jed into the barn but the horse absolutely refused to go under a roof or anything else. It was only in the open corral that he seemed at all at ease. He was used to the plains and knew that nothing living could catch him there.

Jed did not seem in the least distressed by his long race and when he had quieted down a little Scott went in to report on the fire. Heth was not there. He called up the ranger and reported with some heat that the fire had been a fake, and no trace of smoke was to be seen in any part of that region. The ranger only laughed, said it was better to be sure than to take a chance on burning up, and did not seem in the least displeased with the lookout for reporting the fire falsely.

Deprived of the satisfaction of calling down Heth for sending him off on a blind trail, and indignant at the lack of sympathy on the part of the ranger, Scott scraped together a hurried supper, wrote up his diary in rather warm language and went to his bed in an ugly mood.

Nor would it have improved his temper if he could have been up at the ranger station and heard the private conference which was then in session between the ranger and Heth.

CHAPTER VII
SCOTT ESTIMATES SOME SHEEP AND FIGHTS A NEW FRIEND

The next morning Scott determined to see something of the sheep he had missed the day before. He hurried through his breakfast and left the cabin as early as possible. He did not want to be caught by any false fire report or any other restraining orders. He knew that the grazing was the most important work on his district and he knew that he would be held directly responsible for what happened within its boundaries. He therefore determined to find something about it first hand and not have to depend entirely on a subordinate whom he could not trust.

It was a beautiful spring day and to Scott, breathing the clear mountain air and looking out across the glorious sun-bathed valleys, the world seemed a good place to live in. Already he was becoming accustomed to the comparative barrenness of the country and was enjoying the rich coloring of rock and hill which were lacking in his own country. Jed was still a little nervous in the timber but did not show any tendency to bolt as he had the night before.

Scott had studied carefully on his map the ranges allotted to the different herds and knew just how many sheep there should be on each range. He knew that he could locate those ranges and he wanted to check up on the number of sheep, for the supervisor had warned him particularly of the attempt that the stockmen would probably make to run in extras. He had, however, forgotten that it would require four or five days for some of the bands to reach their allotted areas, and he did not realize that it was impossible to count a large number of sheep in the open, or even to estimate them at all accurately without wide experience.

He brought Jed to a sudden stand on the crest of a little knoll and looked with wonder at what appeared to him like a river of sheep on the slope below him. There were not supposed to be any sheep down there. He pulled out his map to make sure and his face fell. A posted driveway crossed the slope at that point and these sheep were on their proper way to their allotted range. He felt not a little disappointed, for he was very anxious to have an opportunity to prove an Eastern man's value and efficiency in enforcing the grazing rules. He knew from experience that he would have to have proof, for there was a tremendous prejudice against him.

He would at least find out whose sheep these were, count them up, and get acquainted with the herder; they might as well know that he was keeping tab on them. He rode down to a knoll which almost overhung the little draw which they would have to take and waited. This would be an ideal place to count them and size them up.

They moved much more slowly than he supposed, but the leaders finally straggled into sight and he began to count. It was easy enough at first. Then a great wave of sheep, the whole width of the draw, hove into sight at once and surged solidly forward. He missed a hundred or so in trying to count the width of the column, and no sooner had he decided that there were about forty sheep abreast than the column suddenly dwindled to about half its former width. He gave up all idea of counting and tried to estimate, but it was no use. Sometimes one side of the column was moving rapidly and the other side standing still. Then all would move uniformly for a second until for some unknown reason the center would shoot suddenly ahead while both sides seemed to be backing up.

"Pshaw," Scott exclaimed in disgust, "you might as well try to count the drops in a whirlpool."

"Jest about," said an amused voice and Scott was startled to find the herder standing beside him.

"Hello," Scott greeted him. "I did not hear you come up."

"Can't hear much this close to that bunch," the herder replied nodding toward the passing sheep.

"No," Scott said, "I thought I would count them as they went past but I had to give it up."

"I reckon so," nodded the herder. There still seemed to be quite a twinkle in his eye.

"They are a fine looking lot," Scott remarked, "How many are there in your band?"

"They counted sixteen hundred and ten in the chute yesterday," announced the herder with an amiable grin.

Scott knew that his permit called for sixteen hundred and the ten extra would not be excluded. The rear of the band was just going by in the charge of a faithful collie.

"Seems like a lot of sheep," Scott remarked absently.

"That's what the permit calls for, ain't it?" the herder cried fiercely. "A government man counted them in, didn't he?"

Scott was surprised at the man's sudden heat. "I guess he did," he answered in a conciliatory tone. "I simply remarked that sixteen hundred was a lot of sheep."

"You can remark all you please but don't accuse me of running in extras. I've got the permit right here in my pocket."

The herder spoke with loud defiance and altogether too much vehemence. Scott felt sure now that there were more than sixteen hundred sheep in that band, but he knew now that he could never count them in the open and he wanted more evidence before he was ready to order them back to the chute for a recount. In the meanwhile he was willing to let the herder believe that he had bluffed him. "Well," he said with well assumed cheerfulness, "the man who counted them knows a lot more about it than I do. So long," and he rode away to see another band, leaving the herder laughing in his sleeve.

Scott rode over to the next driveway and was not long in locating another band. He avoided the mistake he made the first time of catching them in a narrow place and selected an open park for his observations. He waited till the sheep had all spread out contentedly and then rode up to the herder.

"How are they traveling?" he asked genially.

The herder, a surly looking fellow, was slow to answer. He sized Scott up slowly and contemptuously. At last he replied sullenly, "I ain't got no complaint."

In the meanwhile Scott was trying to estimate the band by counting a few and comparing them with the others. "How many are there in this band? Twenty-five hundred?"

"Some guesser," the herder snorted. "There were fourteen hundred in the chute yesterday."

"I'll learn after a while," Scott laughed.

"Fourteen hundred," he exclaimed to himself as he rode past the band, "if there are not more than two thousand there I'll eat them wool and all."

Scott felt certain now that there were too many sheep in these bands, but he wanted to be perfectly sure before he made a move. He visited two more bands and was strengthened in his impression.

"The thing for me to do now," he thought, "is to see sixteen hundred sheep somewhere and find out what they look like."

With this in mind he determined to ride over to the next district and see what the bands looked like over there. His way led through the valley where the fire had been reported the day before. The moist ground and the fresh green brush made him smile with pity for the ignorance of the poor chump up on the lookout who had supposed a fire possible.

"Couldn't start a fire here in a stove," Scott growled.

The words were hardly out of his mouth when he stopped with a jerk. There in a small opening in the trees were the remains of a large bon-fire. He rode over and examined them closely. They were very fresh. The fire had not been out for more than a day for the ground under the ashes was still warm. It was undoubtedly the fire that the lookout had reported the day before. But why had it been built? It was too large for a camp fire. There was no sign of any cutting, so it was not likely that it was built to dispose of logging slash. Moreover it was the only one around there. Scott could not figure it out, but one thing was clear, there had been a large fire and the lookout was not as large a chump as he had thought.

He rode on northward into the next district still wondering vaguely about that mysterious fire. He soon ran into a small band of sheep. The herder was a young fellow, cheerful and evidently glad to see any one who might break the monotony of his lonely life.

"Nice little band you have there," Scott said by the way of introduction.

"You bet," the herder responded enthusiastically, "and she's not so small neither. Of course they would not be so many for the 'red triangle' or some of the other big fellows, but sixteen hundred sheep is a good many for one of us little fellows."

"You don't mean to say that there are sixteen hundred sheep in that bunch, do you?" Scott asked in open-mouthed astonishment.

"Yes, siree," replied the herder in a tone which left no shadow of doubt, "and every one of them paid for with my own money."

Scott saw that some commendation was expected. "Good for you," he mumbled absently, "they're a fine bunch. Luck to you."

He rode on like a man in a trance. There was no doubt about the honesty of this fellow's statement. A herder might be a little careless in estimating the number of his band, but this man owned the sheep himself and had them counted to the last bunch of wool. Scott glanced back once more at the feeding sheep. "Great guns," he exclaimed, "if there are sixteen hundred there, there must be three thousand in each of those other bands." And once more he rode on wondering.

Over the ridge and down in the valley beyond were some more sheep. Again a small band, much smaller than those in his own district. Scott was so absorbed in his own thoughts that he did not stop to think how his abrupt question would sound to the strange herder. "How many sheep are there in that bunch?" he asked gruffly.

"How many do you suppose?" was the sullen answer. "Think I get a permit for fifteen hundred and bring in a dozen?"

The sarcastic answer brought Scott to his senses. "I did not mean it that way," he said. "I don't know anything about sheep and I am trying to learn to estimate them. I was so busy trying to figure it out for myself that I forgot my manners. I had it figured out that there were eighteen hundred there."

"Not on your life," replied the herder angrily, "I only had fourteen ninety-eight when I got up here and the coyotes have gotten two more. There's just fourteen ninety-six and if you demand a recount I'll make you pay for it."

"I have nothing to do with it," Scott replied. "I don't belong in this district. As I told you I am only trying to guess the size of bands."

"Come from district one?" the herder asked, suddenly interested.

Scott nodded.

"Didn't know they even tried to estimate them over there," the herder grinned.

"Maybe they didn't last year," Scott replied coldly as he turned away, "but believe me they are going to be estimated this year and then some."

He knew now that the bands in his own district were outrageously padded, but how under the sun did they get in there? He was doggedly turning the question over in his mind when a faint nicker from Jed warned him that another horse was in sight. He glanced up and saw another patrolman riding rapidly toward him. He was a fine looking fellow and Scott considered himself lucky to meet him. Here was where he might pick up some information which would help him.

"Hello," Scott called in friendly tone as the other came alongside. A nod was the only answer.

"My name is Burton," Scott continued, "I am patrolman in district number one."

"I thought so," said the other without responding to the introduction.

Scott hesitated for a moment but decided to overlook the insult. It might be simply lack of manners. He had offended another man a few minutes before without intending to; maybe this man did not mean it either. So Scott went on, "I rode over here this morning to size up the bands in this district and I was just looking for some one to give me some information." He paused but the other man did not answer.

"Can you tell me why the bands in this district are so much smaller than ours?"

"You ought to know more about that than I do," said the other man coldly.

"How's that?" Scott asked.

"Well," said the other with a contemptuous sneer, "we count ours."

"And we counted ours in yesterday," replied Scott, beginning to get angry at the other's manner.

"Then I suggest that you look in your bank book. That is the only other explanation I can think of."

A dull flush spread quickly under the tan of Scott's face as he slowly dismounted. He stepped coolly up beside the other's horse. His eye was riveted on the other man's face and when he spoke his quiet voice was as cold as steel.

"Are you man enough to get off that horse or shall I pull you off?" he asked steadily.

The other man started as though astonished at the question but sprang lightly from his saddle and stood calmly facing Scott. He was a magnificent specimen, two inches taller than Scott, superbly built, clean cut and a skin that vouched for a well-lived life. Scott did not know that this man was the local idol of the Service men but his practiced eye told him that he had drawn no mean antagonist and he involuntarily sized him up as he talked.

"I came over here," Scott explained coolly, "a stranger to you. I wanted some information. I asked you a civil question, and you answered by accusing me of graft. Your accusation is a lie. Now you can either apologize to me or fight it out."

The man hesitated an instant as though in doubt and then said tersely, "Put 'em up."

They were both on guard in an instant and these two men who had not known of each other's existence five minutes before were fighting like wild men, because of a little misplaced sarcasm.

Scott had superior skill but it was largely offset by the other man's longer reach. They were both in splendid physical condition. Scott was at one disadvantage; he had not been in the mountains long enough to become accustomed to the high altitudes and he breathed with difficulty. He let the other man take the offensive and saved his wind. He received two or three ugly blows from the other's long reach when he thought he was safely out of range, but he was used to punishment and they did not shake him. The other man was not used to such stubborn opposition; he had been undisputed champion of the district too long, and his failure to beat down the other's guard angered him. He saw that Scott's breath was coming hard and he thought to rush him off his feet. He began to swing wildly.

That was just what Scott had been waiting for. When one man loses his temper and the other stays cool the result is a foregone conclusion. Sidestepping a swing that was a little wilder than the others he landed squarely on his opponent's chin with all the weight of his heavy shoulders right behind the blow. The other man's head snapped back with a motion like that of a mechanical toy and he crumpled down into a helpless heap.

It was a mighty blow that no man could have stood up under, but an outdoor man is hard to kill, and the fellow jumped to his feet almost instantly, dazed, but showing a frank smile of admiration.

"Now," thought Scott, "I'll have to look out for him. As long as he stayed mad I knew that I had him, barring accidents, but when a man smiles, look out."

But the fight was over.

"I knew that I ought to have apologized in the first place," the man said with a winning smile, "I was dead wrong and knew it, but I could not resist the temptation to take you on. I acted like a sucker. You knocked me down and the honor is yours. You may think I am yellow for quitting now but the altitude is getting your wind. The old duellers usually stopped at the first blood. I acknowledge myself in the wrong, apologize for all my rudeness and would like to shake hands if you will let me."

Scott grasped his hand eagerly. "I kind of thought you felt that way," he said, "when you hesitated in the first place. Perhaps I was a little quick on the trigger, but I have had that graft business thrown at me so often that I could not stand it any longer."

"Don't blame you a bit. You are a new man and not responsible for your predecessors. Wonder you did not jump me when I insulted you the first time. There was no reason why I should not have responded decently to your introduction, no matter what I may have thought of you. My name is Baxter, Yale '12."

"Well, I am mighty glad to know that there is a white man so close to me here," Scott said earnestly, "for there is something rotten going on in my district and I need some help."

"There certainly has been something rotten in your district in the past," Baxter agreed, "and I'll be mighty glad to help you. Let's eat lunch here under this tree and talk it over."

So the two pugilists sat down on the sunny slope and ate lunch together like long lost brothers.

CHAPTER VIII
A LITTLE DETECTIVE WORK

"How long have you been on the job?" Baxter asked between bites.

"About a week now," Scott replied. "Oh, sure," Baxter exclaimed, "I knew that. Of course we all heard how you bought and rode Jed Clark's horse. He certainly is a beauty. Have you had any trouble with him?"

"No," Scott said, "no real trouble. He ran away with me the other day when a mountain lion got on our trail, but he only took me home a little faster than I intended to go. There does not seem to be a mean trait about him."

"He killed the first man who tried to ride him," Baxter explained. "That gave him the name of an outlaw and kept any one else from trying him. He probably never was mean and only killed the fellow by accident. You were certainly lucky to get him."

And so they talked of little things of purely personal interest, really getting acquainted with each other while they ate their little packages of lunch.

"Now," Baxter exclaimed with a comfortable sigh as he stretched flat on his back and gazed out across the valley, "let's have your trouble."

"Well," Scott began thoughtfully, "I might as well begin at the beginning and tell you the whole story. Then you can judge for yourself. I have mighty little definite to go on and I am too green to understand that."

"Must be something pretty rotten if a greenhorn got on to it in a week," Baxter commented.

"Of course," Scott continued, "the super explained the trouble they had in that patrol district and said he hoped to break it up by getting in a complete stranger from another part of the country. As I did not know anything about sheep they gave me a guard who is an expert, but as I understand it they hold me responsible for keeping the bands down to the number allowed in the permits."

"Who is that guard?" Baxter interrupted.

"His name is Heth."

"Never heard of him."

"I don't like his looks," Scott said, "but I don't really know anything against him. Well, I ran onto the first signs when I went down to visit the small ranchers and find out about the free use stock. Every one of them wanted to know how much it was going to cost him this year, almost dropped dead when I said 'nothing,' and then went with me to the next place to see if I told the same story there. I had quite an escort by the time I got to the last place and they had a regular celebration."

"Of course that was a hang over from last year and has nothing to do with this year's work," Baxter explained.

"Yes, I know that," Scott replied, "but it helps to show you the way I have been worried. The next morning I was to count in the sheep. Just as I was starting out the ranger 'phoned that the lookout had reported a fire on this edge of the district and ordered me out on it because I did not know enough to count the sheep alone. Heth told me the wrong trail and I was more than half a day getting there. When I finally got to the top of that peak over there I could not see the faintest trace of a fire."

"There was one, though," said Baxter with sudden interest, "for I happened to be down this way and put it out. I know who set it, too. It was one of Jed Clark's herders. He said he wanted to burn up the brush so that it would not be in the way of the sheep. Of course I knew that was a fake, but I could not find out why he really did do it, and I could not do anything to him because he had taken great care to keep it from spreading."

"I saw the ashes down there this morning," Scott explained, "and could not figure it out. I did not get back to the cabin till late, all the sheep were in, and Heth was not there. So I decided to come out this morning to see what a band of sheep really looked like and see how they handled them. I visited three or four of them and they looked awfully big to me. I tried to count them, but could not do it. Then I came on over here to see what these bands were like. I have seen a couple of them and they do not look over half as large as mine."

"Is that so?" exclaimed Baxter sitting up.

"Now," Scott concluded, "what I want to know is, how can I tell whether they are really too large? Of course I can order them back for a recount but I want to be pretty sure that I am right before I do that."

"I'll go over with you and have a look," Baxter said, evidently enjoying the prospect. The graft in the neighboring district had always been a source of annoyance and he was glad of the chance to help clean it up. The whole forest considered it a disgrace and a stain on their reputation.

They mounted and rode away together like old friends. Baxter could not keep his eyes off of Jed. "To think," he exclaimed, "that I have been living in the country with that horse for two years and did not have the sense or the nerve to buy him. If you ever miss him you better look in my stable first thing."

It was only a few minutes till they came to one of the bands which Scott had seen in the morning. They were spread out evenly on an open slope and feeding peacefully.

"Now have a good look at that band," Baxter said, "there are sixteen hundred of them. No use trying to count them in the open. It can't be done. You just have to size up a band you know and then compare it with others. It takes a good deal of experience to guess them at all accurately."

"Couldn't a fellow separate them into small groups and count them that way?" Scott asked.

"Ever try it?" Baxter grinned.

"No," Scott replied, "I had never seen more than twenty sheep in one bunch till I came here."

"Well, don't suggest it to a sheep man if you want to look wise. You might as well try to separate a bunch of quicksilver with a pin point. Where the leader goes they all go. You can't separate them."

A little farther on they came to another band. "How many there?" Baxter asked drawing rein on a little knoll above them.

Scott sized them up carefully. They were bunched a little closer than the others and it was hard to judge. "Don't look like quite so many," he ventured a little doubtfully.

"Good," Baxter exclaimed encouragingly, "fourteen hundred. Now for a look at yours."

They rode briskly and Scott whiled away the time with an account of his encounter with the cowboy who tried to steal his horse.

"Jed probably sent him," Baxter said. "I tell you that old scoundrel will do you if he can, and if you throw out any of his sheep he will go to any length to get even."

"They are going out all right," Scott replied firmly, "if I can find any more than the limit. I have a little grudge of my own to even up."

They topped a low ridge overlooking a small plateau and Baxter stopped in sudden amazement. "Great guns," he exclaimed softly as his eye wandered excitedly over a great band of sheep which almost covered the plateau.

"How many?" he asked Scott after a careful estimate.

"Do you mean for me to guess?" Scott asked, "or tell you from my notes how many there are supposed to be?"

"Guess first and look it up afterwards," Baxter suggested.

"Well, judging from the bands over your way I would say that there were at least two thousand, but none of the bands in this district are supposed to be that large." He pulled out his memorandum, "The permit calls for fourteen hundred."

"Gee, but they have their nerve right with them. There are twenty-five hundred in that band if there is one."

"But where did they come from?" Scott asked in perplexity.

"That's the question, all right," Baxter answered thoughtfully. "Possibly another band has gotten mixed up with this one. It is not likely, but we better make sure before we raise a row about it. Where are the other bands?"

"Why not ask the herder?" Scott suggested.

"Because he'll lie like a trooper, and besides we don't want to arouse any suspicions yet a while."

They visited all the bands in the district one after the other and Baxter estimated that each one was carrying from five hundred to twelve hundred more than the permit called for. When they had finished the last examination it was beginning to get dark. The two sat their horses for a moment in silence.

"What's the next move?" Scott asked.

"Wonder how they got in?" Baxter queried.

"I am not so much interested in that right now," Scott answered "as how to get them out."

"Well, if I were you I should first call up Dawson, tell him that you have looked over the sheep, feel sure that there are a large number of extras and suggest a recount. Then it will be up to him."

"You don't think he has been mixed up in this graft in any way?" Scott asked.

"Who, Dawson? Oh, I hardly think that likely. He is considered one of the best rangers on the forest, has always been very strict in our district and is thoroughly disgusted with the black eye this district has always given the forest. What makes you think he is in it?"

"Oh, I don't know," Scott answered uncertainly. "Maybe it is only a hunch, but I have not liked his manner toward me."

"You may be right, but if you are he is a mighty smooth one. I think you are probably mistaken. He has been stung by the patrolmen in this district so often that it is only natural that he should look with suspicion on every new one. Anyway, if you report it to him he will have to do something and your diary will show that you reported it."

"Very well, I'll call him up this evening."

"Then you want to gum shoe around till you find where they got in. That is the first thing the super will want to know and he will expect you to be able to tell him."

"I have never done any detective work," Scott said, "but I'll report to Dawson to-night and get busy in the morning. I certainly appreciate your help. I would have been up against it without you."

"Mighty glad you came over. Sorry I made such a fool of myself this morning, but I assure you that it will not happen again. You don't know how much I appreciate seeing an honest man in this district again. All the boys will be glad to hear the news and will help all they can. So long. 'Phone me how you come out."

"Thanks. Come over again when you get a chance," Scott called after him. "I have a hunch that I am going to be busy here."

He turned Jed's head toward home and rode thoughtfully through the gathering dusk. He told Baxter that he was not interested in how the sheep got in, but now that he knew how to get them out he found himself repeating over and over, "But how could they have gotten in?"

As soon as Jed was safely in the corral Scott called up Dawson, but Mrs. Dawson answered the 'phone and said her husband had not come home yet. Heth was not at the cabin. Scott decided that if Dawson was not at home by the time he had finished supper he would call up the supervisor. He was determined to get some action in the morning. He could not bear the thought of the sheep men thinking that they had hoodwinked him so easily.

While he was washing the supper dishes and still pondering how the sheep got in, the 'phone rang and he found the supervisor on the line. From the tone of his voice he was evidently in no very pleasant humor.

"Burton?" he questioned.

"Yes, sir."

"This is Ramsey. I have just had a report that a large number of sheep have been smuggled into your district up the small ravines to the west of the main road and chute. Do you know anything about it?"

"I know the sheep are there," Scott replied, "I saw them to-day, but I could not figure out how they got in. I did not think they could get them up those cañons."

"Whereabouts are they now and how many of them are there?"

"I visited all the bands in the district to-day and found every one of them running over from five hundred to twelve hundred. Must be four thousand in all."

"Are you sure there was no mistake in the count yesterday?"

There was an emphasis on the "sure" that Scott did not like and he answered with some dignity. "I do not know anything about the counting, Mr. Ramsey. Mr. Dawson ordered me out on a fire early yesterday morning and put Heth in charge of the counting. I have not seen Heth since."

"Why didn't you report those extras?" the voice was hard as steel and Scott knew exactly how he looked.

"I came in only a little while ago, sir. I tried to report to Mr. Dawson at once, but he was not at home. I intended to try him again after supper and then report to you if he was not yet home. I think that a recount should be made at once."

"Dawson was in here this afternoon," Mr. Ramsey replied. "He is the one who reported the rumor to me. I'll take the matter of a recount up with him as soon as he has had time to get home. I am glad that you were able to discover the trespass so promptly. But remember," and the voice was hard once more, "that you are responsible for seeing that no more get in that way. Good-night."

Scott absently hung up the receiver. His jaw was set and his face wore an angry frown for he knew from the tone of the supervisor's voice that he was under suspicion. But the question which had been bothering him was settled. They came up the steep little cañons to the west. Now that he knew that much it would be an easy matter to prevent it in the future and he felt that he could soon prove the suspicions unfounded.

CHAPTER IX
THE MYSTERY OF THE FOUR THOUSAND SHEEP

Early the next morning Scott called up Dawson to find out what his orders would be in regard to the recount. He was itching to serve notice on those herders.

"Good-morning, Mr. Dawson. Did Mr. Ramsey tell you of my report on the number of sheep that are on this district?"

"Yes, he 'phoned me last night. I heard it rumored around among the boys yesterday afternoon and mentioned it to him. How many extras do you think there are?"

"About four thousand altogether."

"How did you count them?"

"Of course I did not count them, but I am sure that the estimate is not far off. Every band will run at least five hundred over."

"Well, if you are sure of that notify those herders to have their bands back at the chute for a recount next.... What day is this?"

"Friday, I think," it was pretty hard for any one to keep track of the days of the week out there in the forest.

"Friday, then tell them to be ready for the recount Monday."

"Not before Monday?" Scott objected with disappointment.

"No, they will have to have that long to get their bands back to the chute and I advise you to check your estimates pretty carefully before you order them back. They will raise some row if you make a mistake. Heth can help you with it."

"I have not seen Heth since I started for that fire day before yesterday," Scott was glad of a chance to report this for he felt that he was getting very little assistance out of Heth and he wanted Dawson to know it.

"Must have gone to town with the checkings," was the unsatisfactory reply.

"Well, I guess I can handle this alone," Scott said, "I am mad enough to do almost anything."

"Go to it then, but be careful not to get yourself into a hole."

It was the most satisfactory conference that Scott had ever had with the ranger and he began to think that Baxter's estimate of him might be right after all. He was going to have the satisfaction of ordering those herders back to the chute and he was not sure that he would have let Heth help him if he had been there. He hurried out to saddle Jed and get started on such pleasant duty. Jed seemed quite as anxious to be off as his master. He came up to the gate at Scott's whistle and they were soon skimming away over the old ridge trail on their joyful errand.

Scott rode straight to the place where he had seen the nearest band the day before. They were nowhere to be seen even when he climbed onto a knoll which gave him a quite extensive view. He was not an expert on sheep, but he had heard from the herders themselves the day before that the sheep had been on very slim rations in the lowlands before they came onto the forest and were now so eager for the fresh spring grass that they were hard to move. There was plenty of grass here and he could not think why they had been moved, or where they could have gone.

But the trail of two thousand sheep is not very hard to find and Scott was soon trotting rapidly along their dusty track. An experienced man would have known from the barrenness of the ground, from which almost all the grass had been eaten or trampled out, that the sheep were bunched and were being driven somewhere rapidly. Scott could not tell this from the trail, but he soon overtook them and found both herder and dog busily engaged in driving the sheep as rapidly as possible down the slope toward the valley cliffs.

It was hard to guess the number when they were bunched that way, but Scott sized them up as best he could and was still convinced that there were too many.

"How many sheep did you say you had in that band?" Scott asked riding up to the herder.

"Fourteen hundred," said the herder.

"They must have swollen since you counted them," Scott replied sarcastically.

"I didn't count 'em," said the herder. "Your man did the countin'."

"I don't think much of the job, whoever did it," Scott retorted. "You have those sheep up at the chute Monday morning and I'll count them myself."

"What, drive these sheep clear back there to that chute just to have them counted again?" the herder screamed.

"Those are the official orders," Scott replied with dignity.

"What are you goin' to do, count them every week? If I run all the fat off these sheep for nothing I'll make it warm for you."

"You won't do it for nothing. It will be a good thing for you. You won't have as many to bother with when you get back."

He left the man cursing and screaming, and rode on. There was intense satisfaction in showing these fellows that he was on to them.

The chase after the second band had brought him so far down toward the valley cliffs that he decided to have a look at the little cañons where the extra sheep had come in before he notified the other herders of the recount. He was still gloating over his little interview with the first herder when he came to the cliffs. He had never seen the cañons but he knew their location from his map and had soon found the one farthest east. He rode clear around the rim of it. There was not a single hoof print. The upper portion of it was rather broad and shallow, but when he went down into it he soon found that it ended in an almost perpendicular drop to the valley below.

"Not much chance there," Scott thought as he mounted Jed and started in search of the next cañon. The second cañon was very much like the first. It was a little larger at the top but ended in the same precipitous drop.

Before he reached the third cañon a new idea occurred to him. Perhaps it would be just as well not to leave any tracks around these cañons. He did not know just why but he had a hunch that he did not want the herders to know that he had been to those other cañons.

He began to suspect that the report was a joke to make him investigate all those impossible cañons.

"I've got to look at every one of them now," Scott fumed, "just to make sure that it was not a fake, but I'll see that nobody knows that I have done it." He rode doggedly on to the next cañon, but he dismounted at some distance from it and took care to cover up his tracks wherever he went. And so he inspected every one of those little cañons along that five miles of valley cliffs, and everywhere he found the same thing. Not a sign of a sheep trail anywhere and the same steep drop at the bottom.

"Self-respecting squirrel would not try to climb any of them," Scott muttered disgustedly as he finished the inspection. "Well, they worked their joke all right but they'll never have the satisfaction of knowing it," and he carefully covered up the last sign of his visit.

"Now to notify those other greasers," Scott exulted as he rode back toward the grazing grounds.

All of a sudden he straightened up with a jerk. He had found out that the entrance of the sheep through the valley cañons was a fake, but if they did not come in there, where under the sun did they come from? He had forgotten all about that in his anxiety to get away from those cañons. There was only one way to find it out now and that was to ride around the boundary of his whole district.

He hurried off to find the other herders for it was a long way around the boundaries and he would have to ride hard if he was to make it before dark. Well, he had the horse to do it. He patted Jed's arching neck affectionately and the big black fellow pricked up his ears in answer.

When he started on his search for the sheep it took him longer than he expected to find the other bands because they had all left the feeding grounds where he had seen them the day before and were for some unaccountable reason moving southward toward the valley cliffs. He did not have time to try to figure it out or even to enjoy an argument with the herder. He simply gave them terse orders to have their sheep at the chute for recount Monday morning without fail and left them cursing the empty air.

No sooner had Scott notified the last herder than he turned about once more and galloped back to the point where the boundary line of his district met the valley cliffs. From there he followed the line northward. From what he had seen of Baxter he did not think it probable that the sheep had come over from his district, but he rode with eyes on the ground determined to draw a complete circle around those bands and not overlook any possible loophole.

He ate his lunch at the same place where he and Baxter had eaten the day before in the hope that he would meet him again but no one came. The same old question which he thought the supervisor had answered for him the day before was still buzzing ceaselessly through his head. How could those four thousand sheep have been spirited onto his district? He had not come any nearer to the solution when he mounted again and started once more on his long search.

The boundary led him far up to the head of the valley and close to the foot of the peak where the lookout tower was located. A steady up grade on a side hill trail finally brought him out on a ridge trail which he knew from the map led from the lookout station to the ranger's cabin. He rode rapidly now but still scanned every foot of the trail carefully.

Jed was keeping a careful lookout too and he shied violently at a little patch of brush beside the trail. Scott glanced back to see what had startled him and reined in with a jerk. A little child was curled up in the shade of the bushes. Jed refused to go near it so Scott dismounted to investigate. It was a little girl about three years old and she was sleeping peacefully.

Scott straightened up to see if there was any one belonging to the child in sight. He could see for a mile down either side of the barren ridge but there was not a sign of life. He did not know the child and could not imagine where she had come from. It was at least three miles to the lookout station and about two miles to the ranger's cabin. He decided to take the child with him and have Mrs. Dawson identify her.

He picked her gingerly up in his arms and started toward Jed. Jed sniffed at her suspiciously and backed away. Scott caught the rein but the horse jerked it indignantly out of his hand and circled out of reach. Jed had never seen a child before and was determined not to carry one until he knew more about it. He let Scott get hold of the rein again, but blocked all his attempts to mount.

Scott looked helplessly down at the child in his arms and found her smiling at him with wondering eyes.

"What is your name, little girl?" Scott asked gently. He was not used to children and was almost as much afraid of her as Jed.

She only gurgled and stretched out her hand to Jed. He sniffed the tiny fingers with a tremendous snort which made the little girl laugh aloud. She was evidently used to both horses and men.

"Aren't you ashamed of yourself, Jed," Scott pleaded. "Why don't you take her on like a good fellow?" But Jed was not reconciled and snorted loudly every time the little hand was extended in his direction.

It was rather exasperating to have to walk and carry a baby with a perfectly good horse trailing along behind, but there was nothing else to do, and the strange procession started for Dawson's. Scott continued to watch for the trail of the sheep and the child amused herself by reaching out to tickle Jed's nose whenever he came within reach. Jed seemed to rather enjoy the game and was fast getting over his scare. The child had seemed light as a feather when Scott first picked her up, but she soon began to get heavy, and he had to shift her frequently from one arm to the other. He was not sorry when the smoke of Dawson's cabin showed about a quarter of a mile ahead. All attempts at conversation with the child had proven fruitless. She only smiled and laughed when he spoke to her.

He had just turned a crook in the trail which brought him in sight of the cabin when he saw a woman run wildly from the gate and start toward him. It was Mrs. Dawson half wild with fright. Scott pointed her out to the child who promptly proved her identity.

"Hurry up, muvver," she called to the already flying figure, "I want to show you something."

"Oh, darling," Mrs. Dawson cried as she snatched the child from Scott's aching arms, "where have you been? Mother has been almost wild about you."

The child only struggled in her mother's arms. "Look, muvver, look," she exclaimed excitedly, and reached once more for Jed's nose. She squealed with delight at the gentle snort.

Her mother snatched her up again and held her fast. "Oh, Mr. Burton," she cried, "where did you find her?"

"Asleep under a clump of bushes about two miles down the lookout trail," Scott explained.

"Two miles! I sent her in to take a nap. I supposed she was asleep, but when I went in the house a little while ago I could not find her. I have run myself half to death looking for her. It is the first time she has ever run away and I was almost frantic."

"She seems perfectly contented," Scott replied. "The horse would not let me ride with her and she has been playing with him over my shoulder all the way home."

"It was awfully kind of you to carry her up and I can never thank you enough." She seemed rather embarrassed, hesitated a moment as though about to say something, but was silent.

"It was pleasure enough to have found her," Scott said as he swung into the saddle, "please don't say anything more about it."

"Do be careful," she called after him excitedly.

"Oh, he's all right now," Scott laughed over his shoulder, thinking she referred to Jed.

He followed the trail down to the chute. Not a track. Not a single sheep track had he seen since he left the valley cliffs. He had made a complete circuit of his boundaries and was absolutely certain that no sheep had entered his district except at the chute. He rode slowly up the trail to his cabin in the gathering darkness trying to analyze the situation. There seemed to be only one solution and yet he hesitated to accept that without even more definite proof than he already had.

As he approached the cabin he thought he saw some one moving about it and he wondered what Heth would have to say for himself, but there was no one there. He put Jed into the corral, ate his lonely supper and settled down to write up a detailed account of the day's work in his diary. He became very much absorbed in the task because he felt that it was extremely important under the circumstances.

Suddenly there was the bark of a revolver and a bullet shattered the window pane above his head. The shock dazed him for a second, but the next instant the angry blood boiled through his veins and sent him tearing out of the cabin to find the coward. He searched the surrounding woods without finding any trace or hearing a sound. He was unarmed and it would have been an easy matter for his assailant to have shot him, but there were no more shots. Scott realized that no man in that country could have missed such a target as he must have presented at the lighted window except intentionally.

"Think you can scare me out of the country, do you? Well, you have another guess coming," and he went doggedly back to the table determined to finish his report.

CHAPTER X
A DISCOVERY

As soon as Scott was dressed in the morning he hurried out to see if he could find any tell-tale tracks of the man who had shot at him the night before. Much to his surprise he found the distinct prints of a horse's hoofs. He had taken it for granted the night before that it was one of the disgruntled sheep herders, but none of them had horses. Then he thought of the horseman who had tried to steal Jed a few days before. He ran anxiously to the corral and was soon reassured by a cheerful nicker in response to his whistle.

All through breakfast he turned over in his mind the problem of the entrance of the four thousand sheep, the warning shot fired by the mysterious stranger the night before and the prolonged absence of Heth. He could not solve any of them to his entire satisfaction, but he came to several important conclusions. He decided that it would be necessary to watch the sheep herders who were in the forest just as closely now to keep them from running the extras off of the forest before the recount, as he would have to do to keep them from bringing other extras on. He also decided to see Baxter and get his coöperation.

He could 'phone Baxter and get him to meet him half way but one could never tell who might be listening in on those party lines and he wanted to keep his business pretty much to himself for the next few days. And so it was that he saddled Jed and rode away to take a chance on finding Baxter, and he thereby greatly disappointed an impatient and anxious gentleman who had been hanging onto a receiver for over an hour hoping to discover his whereabouts.

Jed was feeling very lively that morning and made the gravel fly along the old ridge trail, across the broad valley and up the long slope to the patrolman's cabin on the next district. He was fortunate in catching Baxter just as he was starting out for the day.

"Hello, there," Baxter called gayly, "something doing so soon after sun up?"

"This something started long before the sun got up," Scott replied. "I've started something over my way that looks as though it would keep me pretty busy for a while, and I want to know whether you can help me to carry it through?"

"You bet I can," Baxter cried eagerly, "I'm pining away for lack of excitement. What is it?"

"Well, to begin at the beginning, somebody beat me to the report on those sheep. I had not much more than gotten home the other day after I left you than the super called me up, said that Dawson had told him that the boys had run a bunch of sheep in on me up the cañons in the valley cliffs, and called me down hard for not preventing it."

"Up the cañons," Baxter exclaimed, "I never examined them, but I never supposed that sheep could get up there."

"I told him what I had found out—did not mention you—and he recommended a recount. He said Dawson was on his way home, but he would take it up with him as soon as he had had time to get there.

"In the morning I called Dawson. He told me what he had heard and told me to order a recount Monday morning if I was sure of my estimates, but to be careful or I would get stung."

"I told you Dawson would be all right," Baxter interrupted.

"Yes," Scott admitted, "he was pretty good about it. Well, I took some satisfaction in ordering a recount and thought while I was down that way I would have a look at those cañons. Not a sheep had been up them, and what's more, no sheep ever can get up them. There is a clear drop of three hundred feet at the bottom of each one."

"That's what I thought," commented Baxter, "but if they did not come up there where did they come from?"

"That's what I wanted to know. So I started out right there at the valley cliffs and rode clear around my district looking for sheep tracks. Not a single sheep has come into that district except at the chute."

Baxter gave a long whistle, "What does Heth say to that?"

"He has not been at the cabin since the count. At least I have not see him."

"Looks as though he might be able to explain it," Baxter drawled. "I want to see that man. If he is a sheep man I must have seen him somewhere, but I can't recall the name at all. What is your plan now? Where do I come in?"

"Well, you see I have it figured out this way. I have ordered them up for a recount Monday and they can't get away from that. Probably their next move will be to try to prove that the estimates were wrong and that they did not have any extra sheep."

"Don't let that worry you old man," Baxter assured him, "the estimates I made may not be accurate but they are conservative, and I'd bet my last dollar that every band on your district is padded."

"I am not worrying about your estimates. I am perfectly willing to trust them. What I am afraid of is that they will drive off the extras between now and Monday morning. Then where would I be on the recount?"

"By George," Baxter exclaimed, slapping his thigh, "I had not thought of that. That is certainly what they will try to do."

"That is where you come in," Scott said. "I wanted to see if you would patrol the line here and see that they do not run them over your territory temporarily. They might try that with the idea of bringing them back into my district when the recount is over. They probably figure that I would not dare to order a second recount after they had proved that I was wrong on the first."

"You bet I will patrol that line," Baxter exclaimed eagerly, "both for your sake and mine. I don't want those beggars to slip anything over on me. I have a guard here who is a dandy and the two of us can keep that line tighter than beeswax."

"Are the herders in your district in with that bunch?" Scott asked absently.

"I should say not," Baxter replied contemptuously, "they are a different sort. They come from the other side of the mountains, you know, and hate Jed Clark's gang."

"That's what I thought," Scott said. "How would it do to tell them that you have heard that some of Jed's herders are going to try to sneak some sheep over here and steal some of their grass?"

"Great," Baxter exclaimed. "You are some diplomatist, Burton. I'll tell them and if those fellows do try to come over you want to be around and see the fight."

"Then I'll count on you for this end," Scott explained, "and that will leave me free to watch the chute and keep an eye on them occasionally to see that they do not sneak up over the ridge. That will help me out in great shape. Thanks."

Scott turned Jed toward home and Baxter rode away to warn his herders to be on the lookout for possible interlopers.

Scott thought it safest to go back to the chute before he tried to hunt up the bands. There was nothing to prevent them from driving the sheep back through the chute, if they could get them there without being seen, and it would be difficult if not impossible to prove that they had ever been on the forest at all. The thought made him nervous and he let Jed swing along over the ridge at a lively pace. He stopped at the cabin for a moment but there was as yet no sign of Heth.

"Fine help for me, that fellow is," Scott growled as he rode on down to the chute. "Mr. Ramsey said that he knew all there was to know about sheep. Probably knows all about that extra four thousand, too."

He searched the ground around the chute anxiously. There were no new tracks. Scott heaved a sigh of relief. He felt sure that they would not get by Baxter on the west, they had not crossed the ridge trail to the north, they had not been to the chute on the east, and the valley cliffs were on the south. They must be inside of that quadrangle where they had been the day before, but Scott thought he would drop around that way to see which way they were moving.

He was starting out once more when a snort from Jed attracted his attention to some hoof prints. They were fresh and showed very distinctly in the dusty sheep track. Two horsemen had ridden that way. Instead of following the regular trail up past the cabin to the ridge they had turned westward soon after passing the chute and skirted the edge of the valley cliffs. Scott followed the tracks a little way along the sheep trail but soon lost them when they turned off into the brush. He was not interested in horse tracks, it was sheep that he was looking for.

But he had not gone very far on his way when he pulled up suddenly, hesitated an instant and then rode back to the chute. He dismounted to examine the hoof prints more carefully and straightened up with a puzzled look on his frowning face. Heth's horse had lost a shoe from its near front foot and the tracks in the dust showed the same missing shoe.

"I wonder what he is doing skylarking around this district and avoiding the cabin?" he mused to himself. "Must be that he does not like my company. Well, I am starting out in his direction and may have to force myself on him whether he likes it or not."

He rode slowly forward again, thinking over the question which he was determined to make Heth answer when he finally got him cornered. He followed the dusty sheep trail and kept a sharp lookout both to the south toward the valley cliffs and on the ground, for he wanted to know whether the horsemen kept to the rim of the cliffs or turned north to the ridge trail.

Before long his careful watch was rewarded. The plain hoof prints of a horse crossing the sheep trail from south to north were distinctly registered in the dust. He searched the trail for some distance but there was only the one horse and it was not the one with the missing shoe. The prints had been made only a short time before. In one place where the rider had apparently used the spur the hoofs had gouged deeply into the ground and the bottoms of those tracks had not completely dried out.

"That must mean that Heth is going to stay down there on the bench," Scott thought and he left the sheep trail which was turning slightly to the northwest, so he could keep a better watch on the rim of the cliffs. The forest was open here and by following along the face of the lower slope he could keep a good lookout on the flat bench below. Any one passing that way would be in plain view while he himself would be partially concealed by the forest.

"Maybe I can get a job with a detective agency when I get through with this gum shoe business here," Scott growled to himself. "First you try to keep a man from getting extra sheep onto your district and then you try harder to keep him from getting them off."

It was rather good fun just the same. It was funny, too, to think of Baxter, his guard, himself, and all the sheep herders in the other district tearing madly around the forest to prevent other herders from driving their sheep off of a highly desirable piece of range. He was getting very curious to see just what their scheme would be and how far they would go to hide those extra sheep. Had he known how they came to be on there he would have known that they would go the limit and that a man's life would not be considered too high a price.

Scott was beginning to get a little worried. He had passed half way across his district, crossed two of the areas allotted to two of the bands and had not yet seen a sheep. It looked as though they must be moving to the southwest and he wondered if they could possibly slip by Baxter along the rim of the valley cliffs. Then he thought of the look on Baxter's face when he promised his help, and grinned. "It would be easier for them to hide the sheep in the tree tops," he laughed.

But if that was not the plan, what could it be? Could there possibly be a trail down over those cliffs? It hardly seemed possible that he could have missed it. And yet the scene which unfolded from behind the next shoulder of the slope filled him with wonder and apprehension.

There were the sheep. They looked to Scott like all the sheep in the world. He had thought that his experience with Baxter had taught him something about estimating sheep, but he could not tell anything about a bunch like that. All the bands in the district must have been driven together there. Twelve thousand sheep in one big band. It was a great sight. There were no herders in sight but the dogs were holding the sheep closely bunched. The innumerable bleatings blended into a mighty raucous chorus unlike anything that Scott had ever heard. The band as a whole was stationary but all through it there were little whirlpools of local unrest where small groups were milling around nervously. Every now and then a leader with a few followers would break away from the bunch, but they never went far before they either lost their nerve and dashed wildly back to join the main band or were driven back by the keen-eyed dogs.

There they were, all right, but what under the sun were they doing there? And where were the herders?

The bands were grouped around the heads of two of the largest cañons in the valley cliffs, but Scott remembered very distinctly examining them both carefully. He knew that there was no possibility of getting sheep down through them. They both ended in a sheer drop of three hundred feet to the valley below. He had crawled to the very brink of the cliff and inspected it with great care. He had tried to imagine a man climbing it and had come to the conclusion that it could not be done.

Scott noted a tiny wisp of smoke floating up from the mouth of one of the cañons.

"There is certainly something doing down there," Scott said to himself, "and both my official duty and my own personal curiosity demand an investigation of it."

He dismounted, left Jed in a clump of timber, and walked slowly down toward the cañon.

CHAPTER XI
THE TRAGEDY IN THE CAÑON

The sheep were bunched so tightly around the mouth of the cañon that Scott had to make quite a circle to reach the rim of the cliffs. He then followed the edge of the cliffs back to the cañon which cut back into the plateau like the mouth of a great chute fringed along the sides with aspen. The bottom of it was fairly smooth at the upper end and quite wide, narrowing rapidly and becoming rougher till it ended in the knife-like cut where it broke through the face of the cliff. There it dropped sheer to the valley three hundred feet below.

A queer sight met Scott's astonished gaze when he peered through the screen of aspen down into the little triangular amphitheater. He had no idea of secrecy when he came down there. He had merely wanted to see what was going on and he had walked openly across the bench. It was only the presence of the sheep which had prevented him from walking straight into the mouth of the cañon. But now that he found himself so fortunately located and found the game so well worth watching he nestled quietly down in his screen of aspens and decided to lay low.

He knew now why there were no herders with the sheep. Six men were working desperately building a fence across the mouth of the cañon. Five of them were sheep herders and the sixth was Heth. They were cutting posts from the aspen trees, driving them rather close together, and weaving the tops of the trees between them to form a solid barricade. They had evidently been at the work for some time for the fence was more than two thirds completed. Even then Scott did not understand the significance of it all. Why should they be building a fence across there? There did not seem to be any more reason why the sheep should go down there than over the edge of the cliffs anywhere else.

The voices of the workers floated up to him and he could hear distinctly what they said. It was not long until he heard something which enlightened him on the purpose of the fence.

"This here cache was some idea, Dugan," exclaimed one of the herders who was cutting some brush almost directly under Scott on the side of the cañon.

"You bet," one of the others answered admiringly. "Old Jed couldn't find his own sheep down in here."

So that was the idea. That was the reason all the sheep had been driven down to the cliffs and why no attempt had been made to run them over into Baxter's district or back out the chute. They were going to hide the extras in those cañons till the recount was over and then let them out to graze with the bunch once more. It was a clever idea and would undoubtedly have worked if Scott had not stumbled onto it.

"The question is now," said one of the herders, "can we get enough of them in here? What do you think about it, Dugan?"

Heth answered the question. "Sure we can get them in here. We put twenty five hundred in the other pen and this one is a little larger."

So they already had another cañon fenced and filled. And Heth was in charge of the work. There was no longer any question of how the sheep got into the forest. Heth had let them in. Slowly Scott began to piece together the evidence. How did they know that Heth and not himself was going to count those sheep? Then he remembered how Heth had delayed things that morning and how relieved he had seemed when the telephone rang reporting the fire. And Heth had sent him on the wrong trail purposely, so that he would have time to get in all the sheep and have them well away from the chute before Scott could get back.

There his train of evidence broke for a second. Who else was in the game? How did Heth know that fire would be so promptly reported? Then he recalled that it was one of Jed Clark's men whom Baxter had caught setting an apparently purposeless fire on that very morning. He himself had seen the traces of it. It was certainly a deep laid plot. He saw now how the cards had been stacked against him by a cunning hand and he knew now why he had taken such a violent dislike to Heth.

He wondered if his hunch to distrust Dawson was as reliable. There was certainly no evidence against him as yet. The fire had been reported to him honestly enough by the lookout and he had simply given the necessary orders. It was perfectly natural that he should have sent Scott to look after the fire and left a sheep man to look after the sheep. Moreover, Dawson was in charge of Baxter's district also. There never had been any trouble over there and Baxter thought he was all right. The ranger also stood very high in the judgment of the supervisor, who had had years of opportunity to size him up. No, he must have been mistaken about Dawson, but he chuckled to think how well he had judged Heth.

These discoveries did not make him like Heth any better but he certainly admired his nerve. How did he know that Dawson or some of the others would not drop in there to inspect the counting of the sheep? Yes, it had certainly taken plenty of nerve and Heth seemed to have it.

In the meanwhile, the fence building was progressing rapidly. When they came to the side of the cañon for posts or brush Scott caught an occasional remark, but the work kept them out too far most of the time. From what little he did hear he knew that they considered their plan a big success and a tremendous joke on the greenhorn patrolman from the East.

At last the fence was completed all except a narrow opening which was to serve as a gate. There was nothing more to do but drive in the sheep. The herders looked with satisfaction on their work and rested from their exertion while Heth gave the fence a final inspection. He pronounced it good and ordered them to bring in the sheep. Scott was wondering what had become of the horse he had been trailing when Heth led him out of a clump of aspen near the bottom of the cañon. He passed almost directly under Scott and a herder who had come over there to get a coat which he had laid aside called to him, "Where is the greenhorn now, Dugan?"

Scott started at that name addressed directly to Heth. He had heard them speak to Dugan before and he had heard Heth answer to it, but he had thought that Heth was simply volunteering an answer to a question addressed to another man. Now there could be no question about it; there was no one else there. Even the man's name was a fake. No wonder Baxter had never heard of him.

Scott itched to jump down there on them and show them where he was, but he realized now that it would be neither safe nor politic. He must let this thing go till he had counted the sheep out through the chute. Then would be the time to disclose his discovery. He could not prove anything now. He had no witnesses to what he had heard and there was no regulation to prevent the herders from penning some of their sheep up in the mouth of the cañon if they wanted to do so. He must wait.

Dugan's answer made him chuckle. "He's over getting some pointers from Baxter on estimating bands of sheep."

"He'll go back and take some more when he gets through counting ours to-morrow," the herder laughed.

Dugan rode through the gate and over to one side of the fence. "Drive them in now, boys," he called. "I saw Dawson this afternoon and he said he would have Mr. Ramsey up for the recount so that we could rub it into the greenhorn right. He won't last long after that."

Scott smiled when he thought what a jar their plans for his disgrace were going to get. Then his forehead wrinkled in wonder. If Dugan had seen Dawson this afternoon as he said, it must have been Dawson's horse which he tracked from the chute over to the ridge. It looked as though the ranger must know what was going on.

Dugan had started to ride away when one of the herders called after him, "Has Jed seen Dawson yet about that reservoir?"

"No," Dugan shouted back, "but Dawson promised to 'phone me to-night and say where he would meet him." Dugan rode rapidly away toward the chute and the herders prepared to pack the sheep into the enclosure.

Scott watched the proceedings with interest. It was his business to learn as much as possible about handling sheep and this looked like a good opportunity. Moreover he could not get out of there now without being seen and secrecy had become important.

One of the herders walked out to the sheep, picked out an old bellwether and led her quietly down toward the cañon. Scott had expected a great deal of excitement, but the old sheep walked along peaceably enough and all the others streamed along behind. The leader once inside the others crowded eagerly to get through. One of the herders stood beside the gate and made a rough estimate as they rushed past.

In half an hour the cañon was filled with a seething mass of nearly three thousand sheep. The brush gate was dropped into place and the cache was complete. Dugan had over-estimated the size of the cañon. They were packed in so tightly that some of them were forced far down into the neck of the cañon within twenty feet of the valley below. The herders had taken the precaution to block that narrow opening with a pile of brush but the sheep seemed to know that it was there and instinctively crowded away from it.

The excessive crowding and the excitement of the sheep outside that could not get through the gate made those inside nervous. They milled around restlessly, crowding now in this direction and now in that. It seemed to Scott that some of them must inevitably be trampled to death. There was a perfect bedlam of noises.

At last the herders with the aid of the dogs finally succeeded in driving those outside the fence away and the excitement subsided a little. Fortunately the bands were headed east along the open bench and did not go back into the timber where they would have seen Jed. One of the herders stayed behind to see how the prisoners would behave.

Scott was beginning to wonder how he could get out of there without being seen when he saw one of the other herders coming back. The two consulted together for a moment but the noise of the sheep made it impossible for Scott to hear anything. The newcomer then came over to the end of the fence next to Scott, scrambled over it and began working his way along the side of the cañon on top of the talus slope at the foot of the wall. It was uncertain footing. Stones rolled from under his feet and frightened the already excited sheep. Little groups began bolting this way and that and piling up their neighbors.

The man was almost directly under Scott before his purpose became apparent. It was only another case of a forgotten coat. The man was swearing volubly at the slippery talus. He put on the coat for easier carrying and started crawling back. Twice he slipped and only saved himself from tobogganing down into the sheep by the aid of a friendly stump. The third time he braced his foot against a large bowlder. The shale under the bowlder crunched ominously for a second. The bowlder trembled, slid a few feet with the sliding shale and then rolled bounding down into the mass of frightened sheep.

The crazed animals struggled madly to get away, they only succeeded in piling up on those immediately around them. Scott shut his eyes as the great bowlder crashed relentlessly into the writhing mass. The cries of the injured animals put terror into the rest and they milled around wildly, trampling each other down, and scrambling over the backs of others.

Suddenly the mass surged down the cañon and two or three on the lower edge, maddened with fright, dashed over the pile of brush and disappeared over the edge of the cliff.

Even the thought of an injured animal had always seemed horrible to Scott. The sight of a starving cow he had once seen had haunted him for days. Now the thought of those poor animals dashed to pieces on the rocks below made a great lump rise in his throat. The sight that followed sickened him.

No sooner had those three sheep disappeared over the edge of that pile of brush than the others streamed madly after them. The first rush swept the brush pile over the edge and that great mass of sheep poured after it. They crowded into the narrow neck of the cañon as though it had been a stable door and plunged over the edge of the cliff without the slightest hesitation.

Scott lay in his little clump of aspens paralyzed with horror. His body and limbs seemed to turn to ice, he could not move them. He wanted to cry out to the herders who could not see what was happening from where they were. He wanted to look away from that awful sight, but he could neither shout nor turn his head. He just stared with glassy eyes and horror in his heart.

The herders could not see past the neck of the cañon from where they were, but they knew sheep and with the first wild rush down the cañon they realized what was taking place. They scrambled madly along the edges of the cañon, fighting their way toward that narrow pass. Desperately they tried to stem that fatal tide. They might as well have tried to push back the tide of the ocean. One of them was nearly swept over the edge by the living stream. Rapidly and inevitably the big band sifted through that narrow pass like the sands of the hour glass.

Only a hundred of them were left. The men made a last frantic effort to head them off. They succeeded in turning them for a second, but only for a second. The bewildered sheep stopped for an instant, made a wild rush and disappeared after the others. One of the herders dived desperately into the bunch and succeeded in catching a small ewe. She struggled violently and the herder, exhausted by his exertions, lost his hold. The ewe seemed dazed at first and trotted a few steps up the cañon, but she quickly got her bearings and dashed wildly over the cliff.

The two herders lay alone on the trampled floor of the little cañon, exhausted, dazed by the sudden tragedy which had befallen them, and gazed despairingly at each other.

Scott felt like a man coming out of a trance. He passed his hand absently over his eyes. His forehead was clammy with a cold perspiration. He felt sick. Not a sound came from the valley below. The silence of death in the little cañon seemed uncanny after the pandemonium of the moment before. He could not think, he had no plan; he did not know where he was going; he just had a wild desire to get away from that loathsome place.

Shudderingly he backed out of that little clump of aspen and staggered blindly toward the forest.

CHAPTER XII
THE INTERCEPTED MESSAGE

When Scott realized where he was he found himself sitting in the shade of the pines beside Jed. The horse seemed to realize that something was wrong. He was standing close with his soft muzzle almost resting on his master's shoulder. For one wild moment Scott thought that he might have been dreaming, but the dirt on his shirt where he had been lying in the aspens and the vividness of the picture soon forced him to accept it as a reality.

Watching the fate of that great mass of sheep was the most tragic experience of his life. It seemed to him like a personal catastrophe. Certainly this would put a stop to any further attempts on the part of the stockmen to evade the laws. Judged only as a financial problem the loss of that band would cost Jed Clark more than he would have gained by crowding on all the extras that the range could possibly support under any conditions. And to Scott the financial loss was the smallest part of it; to him it appeared more in the light of a crime.

His first impulse was to ride directly down to the supervisor's office and report the whole affair, taking it for granted that the horrible accident would make Jed Clark penitent and cause him to give up the fight. Fortunately, however, he did not act upon the impulse. Instead he tried to analyze the case as coldly and logically as he could. After all, would Jed feel as he did? He knew that Jed was not very soft hearted. His experience in the horse trade had taught him that much. Moreover, he knew that most of these men looked on sheep as values in wool and mutton rather than animals, and would probably look on the death of those poor beasts as so many dollars to be charged off to profit and loss. It would make Jed even more determined than ever to make good his loss by any means within his reach. No one but his own men knew of his loss and he had the extra sheep in the other cañon to conceal.

The more Scott thought about it the clearer it became to him that it was his duty to push the case right through to a finish as he had been doing before the accident. After all, he had no proof against Jed as yet and would not have until the recount had been made and he had shown up the hidden sheep. He had heard and seen enough to convict a dozen men, but he had only his own word for it and he felt sure that he, a stranger, could not make himself believed as against Dawson, an old timer with a good record in the service. No, he must push the thing through, and he must be about it.

He glanced at his watch. It was almost four o'clock. He did not think there was much danger of their trying to move the sheep out of the cañon, but he decided to have Baxter watch them. He wanted his advice anyway. He would be a good witness, too, and anything he could learn from the herders would help to back Scott's testimony.

With a final glance at the scene of the tragedy he mounted and rode swiftly away in search of Baxter. He guessed rightly that he would find him patrolling the boundary of his district. There was no trace of him but he followed his hunch to turn to the left and soon ran onto him.

"Nothing doing here," he shouted as soon as Scott was within shouting distance. "Any news over your way?"

"Is there?" Scott exclaimed, "there's nothing but news and I need some more help from you."

"Good, I hope you have a more lively job for me this time. Things have been pretty dull here, even for a Sunday afternoon."

Scott had been so intent on his problem that he had forgotten it was Sunday. He had even forgotten that he had not had any lunch.

"It may not be any more lively, but I think maybe it will be more interesting," he explained. Then he proceeded to tell Baxter how he had found the sheep, and how he had watched them build the fence. Baxter listened eagerly and in silence for fear he would interrupt the story, till Scott came to the discovery of Heth's real name.

"Dugan!" Baxter exclaimed excitedly. "Did you say he was a thin, wiry fellow, medium height, dark hair, and a rather sharp face?"

"That's the man," Scott said, "Do you know him?"

"Know him," Baxter exclaimed excitedly, "I know him like a book. I thought that I knew all the sheep men in this country and I know him. Why man, he used to be Williams' foreman over on the Onama when they had all that trouble over there. He's a gun man and a crook from the word go."

"He's a crook, all right," Scott said, "whatever else he is. And what's more I believe that Dawson is in with him."

"Oh, he can't be," Baxter remonstrated, "and yet, hold on. He knows Dugan as well as I do and he must have appointed Dugan for this job."

Scott told of the proposed meeting that evening between Dawson and Jed Clark.

Baxter gave a long whistle. "It would be interesting to know what goes on at that meeting."

"And that is exactly what I am going to find out. But I did not tell you the worst of this cañon business."

Scott felt the horror of that awful sight coming over him again as he told the story and Baxter listened with open mouth.

"The poor fools," Baxter exclaimed sympathetically. "It's just like them though; one go, all go. You say there were about three thousand of them? Well, they ought not to be so hard to count now."

The cold-blooded remark made Scott realize how well he had guessed what Jed's attitude would be. If it did not affect Baxter any more than that it would roll off Jed like water off a duck's back.

"What's your plan now?" Baxter asked.

"Well, Dugan said Dawson was going to 'phone Jed to-night where he would meet him and I am going to listen in and see if I can find out where that meeting is going to be. If I succeed, I propose to be there and see what happens."

"Where do I come in?" Baxter asked curiously.

"I wanted to see if you would watch those sheep over there in that cañon and see if you can overhear any more of the conversation between those two herders. We'll need all the evidence we can get and besides I want to be sure that those sheep will be there when I come down to show them up to-morrow after the recount."

"Sounds interesting," Baxter grumbled. "Well, it can't be any worse than watching this line. I'll go get some blankets and hike down there."

"I certainly shall appreciate your help," Scott said. He knew that it was not the kind of a job that Baxter would most like but he felt confident that he would do it.

"Oh well," Baxter replied cheerfully, "I'm just as anxious to see Jed Clark cleaned up as you are and I'm glad enough to do anything to help. I only hope they try to take them out of there. There might be some excitement then. I'll see you to-morrow when you come down to prove up. Luck to you on your mission to-night."

"Thanks, wish you could be there."

There was nothing to do now but to hurry back to the cabin and see if he could intercept that telephone message. It did not seem to be essential to his case to know what happened at that meeting. As Baxter had said Dawson must have approved Heth's appointment and it would be easy enough to prove that he knew who Heth really was. Nevertheless, Scott wanted to sift the thing to the bottom now that he had started on it and he felt that his own success in the service would depend on cleaning up the whole situation. He was getting a little nervous. Dugan had said that Dawson would call in the evening but that was a vague term, and he might be too late to catch the message. It was never any trouble to get speed out of Jed. He loosened the rein a little and the big horse fairly flew. He seemed to delight in those wild runs over the mountain trails.

Scott knew that sounds traveled far in the stillness of those mountain forests, and he thought it best to approach the cabin cautiously. He pulled Jed down to a walk long before he reached the cut off to the cabin and turned down through the woods instead of following the stony trail.

It was still light enough to see. When he came within sight of the cabin he stopped and watched for some time. There was no sign of life. He rode quietly up to the cabin door and pushed it open. There was no one there. He hurriedly put Jed in the corral, ran up to the cabin and cautiously took down the receiver of the telephone. All was quiet. He hung up the receiver and started to get some supper. He was beginning to realize that he had not had anything to eat since breakfast.

He had not relished this detective business at the first, but he was beginning to like it now, and his wits were alert to every move that the enemy might make. A new thought occurred to him. It was a dangerous thing for a ranger to make a secret date with a crooked stock man over the telephone, especially over a party line. If these two were as thick with each other as he suspected, would they not have some way of talking over the 'phone without ringing up? A set time or something of that kind?

It was only a hunch, but it took such a strong hold on Scott that he abandoned his supper preparations, grabbed some biscuits and sat down at the 'phone. Cautiously he took down the receiver once more. All was still, but with a look of grim determination he held the receiver to his ear with one hand while he handled the biscuits with the other.

It was a long chance he was taking but he felt it was the only safe way and he hung on. The 'phone rang once or twice and he listened to several long conversations between the ranger's wife and the wife of the man at the lookout station and with a woman somewhere in the town. They seldom had a chance to see their neighbors and these long telephone conversations took the place of personal calls. Scott learned more about the ills of children and the multiplicity of petty troubles that worry a house-wife than he had ever dreamed of. It seemed to him that those conversations would be endless.

"Fine figure I am cutting here," he thought, "if they have had their little talk before I came." His arm cramped from holding up the receiver. He tried the other one and devised all kinds of schemes for propping it up. It seemed as though he simply could not hold it any longer.

"Oh what's the use," he exclaimed aloud after two hours' struggle with the thing, "they probably did their talking before I came. Or Dawson may be in town now calling him up over some other line." But it was his only chance and he hung on.

He shifted the receiver to his left hand for the twentieth time and tried to write up his diary with the other. It worked fairly well. His hand was numb but seemed to have frozen into position. He had become thoroughly absorbed in recording the exciting incidents of the day as accurately and vividly as he could when his ear caught a faint click in the 'phone. He almost stopped breathing. Nothing more followed and he had about concluded that he must have been mistaken when there was another faint click.

There was another long silence while Scott waited in tense expectation. He felt absolutely certain that Dawson and either Jed Clark or Dugan were on the line listening to make sure that the coast was clear.

A quiet voice which he instantly recognized as Dawson's said casually, "The fire was in the cañon a half mile below the chute was it?"

"Was at half-past ten," answered another voice in the same tone.

A short period of silence followed by two faint clicks announced that the conversation was over. Scott intended to hang up as carefully as they had, but when he moved his hand it flumped down on the table with a bang as though it did not belong to him. The noise startled him so that he jumped to his feet as though to defend himself. Then he laughed at himself for he realized that it was only his over wrought nerves, that the other parties had both hung up, and that he was alone on a mountain several miles from anywhere.

So the meeting was to be in the cañon a half a mile below the chute at half-past ten. He was so tickled with his own success that he felt like shouting aloud. He knew exactly how a detective must feel when an indefinite clew leads him straight to the mark. But he also knew that there was a hard job ahead of him that night and a long day coming to-morrow, so he suppressed his desire to celebrate and fried some bacon instead.

CHAPTER XIII
THE SECRET CONFERENCE

While Scott finished his supper he planned carefully what he would do that evening. It would be no simple matter to locate that meeting place and get near enough to it to see and hear without being detected. At first he thought it would be best to go early and wait for the others, but he did not know exactly where it was to be and he did not know when Jed might get there. If Jed happened to get there before he did and saw him come snooping along he did not know exactly what would happen, but he felt pretty sure that he would not be in at the meeting. No, the safest plan would be to wait till Dawson had gone down the trail and then follow him.

Scott washed the dishes, finished up his diary and reports and straightened up the cabin. He glanced at his watch. It was just nine o'clock. He cast about for something to do, for he did not feel so nervous when he was busy, but he decided that nerves or no nerves the thing for him to do was sit quietly down and try to think of every contingency that might arise.

He pictured the situation as accurately as he could. He planned how he would try to approach them if they were in the open, or in the brush. He thought out just what he would say and do if they discovered him when he was coming down the trail or when he was eavesdropping on the conversation. He became so absorbed in it that he forgot all about his nerves.

He looked at his watch once more. Nine-thirty. Dawson might come along any time now. Suddenly it occurred to him that Dawson might come by the cabin to make sure that he was there. That would make it awkward. It would be very hard to get out of the cabin unnoticed without waiting so long after Dawson left that he might lose him. He decided to leave at once and wait for Dawson at the chute where the two trails met. Then he would be sure to see him whether he came by the cabin or not and it would not be so hard to follow him.

For a moment Scott looked uncertainly at the revolver hanging on the wall. He felt that he might need it to-night, but he had never carried one and he did not like the thing. His father's coachman, an ex-prize fighter, had given him innumerable boxing lessons and he was not afraid of a fist fight with any man, but he did not like the idea of shooting a man. If he happened to hit a man—the chances of his doing so were not very good—he knew that he would always regret it and would keep wondering if it had really been unavoidable. He decided to leave the revolver.

There were no other preparations to make. He stuffed his flashlight into his pocket as an after thought, left the lamp burning as though he had just stepped out for a moment, and walked casually out of the cabin toward the wood pile. If Dawson were passing, it would be just as well that he did not see him walking down the trail. Once in the shadow of the woods he stopped and listened intently for some minutes. If there was any one else around he must have been doing the same thing for he could hear nothing. He circled around by the corral at the risk of a nicker from Jed and struck the trail once more well below the cabin. He walked carefully, avoiding the noisy gravel and arrived at the chute without accident.

Scott crawled into a little clump of aspens and settled down to wait. He had been doing so much of this hiding in the past few days that he began to feel like a sneak thief. It was a beautifully clear starlit night and cool as the nights in that high altitude always were. Scott missed the myriad night noises of the North, especially the incessant hum of the mosquitoes and other insects. Here there was not the buzz of a single wing. What few noises there were sounded strange to his Northern ear. The sharp yap of the coyote replaced the full throated bass of the timber wolf. He missed the weird cry of the loon and the sullen squawk of the blue heron. An almost imperceptible breeze set the aspen leaves to whispering softly.

Scott loved these night noises. Several nights at the cabin he had sat out in the open and listened to them a while before going to bed. Now they served to while away the time and break the monotony of his anxious vigil. He kept a sharp lookout on the junction of the trails and listened intently for he wanted to make certain whether Dawson had come by the cabin.

He was listening to the far away barking cry of a pack of coyotes on the trail of game, probably a rabbit. The sound rose and fell as the quarry led them up onto a ridge or down behind a hill, and almost died away altogether when the trail doubled back into some deep, spruce-filled cañon. He could almost see the chase and could tell whether they were gaining on their prey or losing ground. They were gaining now, gaining fast, probably with their victim in plain sight. The yaps were coming fast and furious and he expected them momentarily to break off with a snarl of triumph which he probably could not hear but would know was there.

Suddenly a faint click far up the trail in the direction of the cabin made him lose all interest in the distant chase. He listened tensely and caught the sound again. It came again, nearer this time, and soon he could hear the continuous clatter of steel hoofs of a pacing horse on the loose gravel of the trail. Dawson was coming and there was nothing silent or secret about the way he came. There was a difference between talking conspiracy over a public 'phone and riding over his own district where he could account for his presence in a thousand ways. In fact no one had the right to challenge him there at all. It suited Scott all right. The more noise Dawson made the easier it would be to follow him.

The horseman passed through the chute and so close to Scott that he instinctively shrank back although he knew that he could not be seen. But he had forgotten the horse's nose in laying his plans. The animal gave a snort of fear and shied violently. It might have led a more curious or less preoccupied man to stop and investigate, but Dawson did not seem to be at all suspicious. Indeed, he seemed to be so absorbed in his own thought that he hardly noted the actions of his horse.

Dawson's apparent indifference reassured Scott. As soon as he was sure that he could not be seen he slipped from the shadows and followed as swiftly and noiselessly as he could. When hidden by a bend in the trail he ran, in the straight stretches he was obliged to drop farther back. The cañon was steep and the pace was slow enough to make shadowing rather easy. There did not seem to be any hesitation on Dawson's part. He seemed to know exactly where he was going and Scott gained the impression that there had been such meetings before in a place well known to both parties. This impression was strengthened when Dawson reined in so suddenly that he almost ran onto him at a sharp bend, listened a second, and rode confidently into the scattered brush beside the road.

Scott listened a moment. He could still hear the horse going so he ducked into the brush and followed. Yes, it was evidently a well known meeting place. Dawson could not expect to be found away back in there except by some one who knew the way. At last the horse stopped. Scott listened for voices. Probably Jed had not arrived for he could not hear anything. He thought it safest to circle the spot and sneak up from the other side; he did not want Jed to stumble over him.

The experience up the trail with Dawson's horse had taught him a lesson. He remembered that a horse has very keen eyesight, could see in the dark, and could also hear and smell much better than a man. It would be necessary to steer clear of the horses. He circled far out to the left and crawled as cautiously as an Indian. A turned over stone or a slip of any kind might be fatal to the whole enterprise now. It was slow, tiresome work, but intensely exciting. When the slope of the ground and the stars told him that he was about opposite the place where he started he slowly closed in on the trail. He was moving almost by inches now and stopping every few feet to listen. There was not a sound to guide him.

Suddenly Dawson struck a match to light his pipe. It was not more than fifteen feet to one side. It seemed to Scott like a coast defense search light. He could see Dawson so plainly, sitting comfortably on the ground with his back against an aspen tree, that it seemed as though Dawson must see him. He crouched as flat as he could and would have dug into the ground if he had been a badger. It never occurred to him that the match had effectually blinded Dawson to everything around him. It made him shudder to think that if his direction had been a little more accurate he would have been right on top of that silent figure before he struck the match.

Scott started backing up inch by inch to avoid the possibility of getting in Jed's path. He had hardly gained what he considered to be a safe position when he heard the soft thud of unshod hoofs and saw a dark shadow looming up through the brush in the direction of the trail. He had become so accustomed to the starlight that he could see pretty well now. The newcomer rode straight toward the little tree where Dawson was sitting, dismounted about twenty feet away and strode over there.

It was Jed Clark, and Scott could see, even in that uncertain light that he was in an ugly mood.

"Fine night for a party," Dawson ventured by way of greeting.

Jed answered with a burst of profanity. "Fine mess that saintly patrolman of yours has gotten us into, too. That fellow is too good for this world and if I get a good chance I'll send him up where he belongs."

"Pshaw, what are you fussing about. This recount is the best thing that ever happened. I saw Dugan to-day and he said they had the sheep hidden as snug as a bug in a rug."

"They're hidden, all right," Jed sneered.

"Then why worry? After the recount we can trot them out again and we'll be stronger than ever. Nobody will have the nerve to order another recount for some time."

"You may 'trot out' some of them after the recount, but there's others you won't."

The bitter sarcasm in Jed's tone made Dawson sit up in alarm. "What's up?" he asked anxiously.

"A lot you don't seem to know anything about," Jed retorted angrily. "We lost three thousand sheep this afternoon, that's what I'm fussing about."

"Lost them? How?"

"Through that cursed patrolman of yours, that's how." Jed was so angry that he was almost beside himself.

"Didn't eat 'em did he?" Dawson sneered.

"Can now if he wants to," Jed raved, "they're dead enough to eat."

"Dead?" Dawson ejaculated.

"Yes, dead! What did you think I meant? Lost in the brush?"

"Don't be a fool, Jed," Dawson answered quietly, "you are acting like a crazy man. If the sheep are dead it cannot be helped now, but I would like to know how it happened."

Jed finally told the story of the lost sheep, interrupted at frequent intervals by uncontrollable bursts of profanity.

Dawson listened calmly. "How do you know this?" he asked.

"Bob left Sancho up there to watch the sheep in the other cañon and came down to tell me. Nine thousand dollars gone to smash in one afternoon and all through that—"

"Don't get to raving again," Dawson interrupted. "It's tough luck but we can both stand it."

At this confession of partnership Scott's eyes popped wide open with amazement. He had already suspected Dawson of levying graft money for allowing extra sheep on the forest but such a far-reaching fraud as this had never occurred to him.

"We could stand it, yes, but I'm not going to."

"What do you mean?"

"I mean that I am going to own up to running on some extras, let 'em cancel my permit if they want to, and get into some more profitable game."

"You talk like a baby," Dawson answered coldly. "You know how much we have made out of this thing in the past and how much more we can make in the future, and you talk about throwing up the whole thing just for one stroke of bad luck. Now listen to a little reason. If you give up now, all those sheep, including the twenty-five hundred in that other cañon, will have to be sold on a losing market. Nobody knows anything about this except our own men. We'll put the recount through to-morrow, clean up all suspicion, and carry the twenty-five hundred extras through the summer. Then if you still want to get out we can sell to a good market in the fall. That's the sensible way to do it."

"Have it your way, then," said Jed sullenly, "but remember this. If you don't get rid of that patrolman inside of ten days I'll blow the whole thing, so get busy." He rose as though he had delivered his ultimatum and was ready to leave.

"I'll attend to Burton," Dawson answered quietly. "There will not be much trouble in getting rid of him after he falls down on that recount to-morrow. Now we'll settle those accounts."

"We'll settle those after you get rid of that patrolman," Jed answered doggedly.

"We'll settle them now," Dawson answered coldly.

"Don't try to bully me," Jed flared angrily, "if I say the word you know what they will do to you."

"Yes," Dawson answered contemptuously, "I'd lose my little job, but I doubt if I'd starve. It might be different with you, considering the mortgage I hold on your ranch. According to my figures you owe me two thousand dollars on the business of the last six months."

Jed sullenly handed over some papers. "Don't be pushing me too far with that mortgage. It's not recorded, you know."

Dawson ignored the threat. He had gained his point and was ready to smooth down his victim's feelings. "Well, I did not mean to rub it in, Jed. You and I have too good a thing in this business to fight with each other. I'll attend to this end of the business and I know from experience that you can handle the other end. I'm going to have the super up for that recount in the morning and we'll rub it into that incorruptible dude in fine shape. Better come up and see the fun."

"I'll be there, all right," Jed replied, very much mollified. "I wouldn't miss seeing him taken down for considerable. I'd pretty near be willing to drive the other twenty-five hundred sheep over the cliff to make sure of it."

They mounted and rode slowly out to the trail, all signs of the quarrel wiped away by the cunning hand of the ranger.

Scott listened until he heard the hoof beats die away in the distance and then walked slowly back to the cabin thinking of the wonderful surprise party he was preparing for those two in the morning.

CHAPTER XIV
THE RECOUNTING OF THE SHEEP

Scott walked slowly back to the cabin thinking of the tremendous pow wow there would be when he sprung his discoveries the next day. He felt sure that neither the supervisor nor any one else outside of the ring, unless it was the small ranchers who had been using free range, had ever suspected Dawson. Every one knew that Jed Clark would beat any one he could, but with Dawson it would be a different matter. He had the reputation, both in the service and outside for sterling honesty and for strict enforcement of the regulations. He would have felt sorry for him if he had not overheard his cool schemes that night for getting rid of the "Eastern dude." Now he looked forward with pleasure to the stir his disclosure would make.

He approached the cabin as he had left it by way of the corral and the wood pile, for he thought possibly Dawson had stopped there again on the way home. He glanced quickly around the cabin. There was no one there, but there was a piece of paper lying on the table in a conspicuous place near the lamp. It was a scribbled note from Dawson.

Dropped in but did not have time to wait for you. We'll have the recount to-morrow morning about ten o'clock. Ramsey is coming up and I'll be down there. Probably Jed will be up to count for his side. A recount is rather a serious matter and I hope for the good of the Service that you have not made any mistake.

Hastily,
DAWSON

"I hope you have not made any mistake," Scott repeated with a grin. "That's a pretty slick little piece of sarcasm and I'll bet he grinned when he wrote it, but if he knew what I know he would have made it a prayer that I had made a mistake."

In order to have his records complete he finished up his daily diary report with a detailed account of the evening's interview. It was one o'clock when he blew out the light and rolled into bed. He was so tired with his long day's work that he went to sleep before he had planned out the details for the next day as he had intended.

However, he did not oversleep himself the next morning. He finished breakfast early and put the cabin in apple pie order in case he should have any official visitors before the recount. He had an idea that no one would have much time for the inspection of cabins after that.

He determined to ride out and see that the herders were bringing up the sheep according to his orders. He found Jed ready to go as usual and was soon trotting along gayly through the forest. The sun was shining brightly and his mood was in keeping with the day. He felt that his triumph was sure and he had no misgivings. He had not gone very far when he ran onto one of the bands headed for the chute.

It was feeding time for the sheep and they were in no hurry to travel. They moved by jerks, those in front hanging back till they were pushed on by those behind. Then they would trot a little way and stop to eat once more. Those in the center kept trying to push out to the sides where they could find some grass, and it kept the herder and the dog both busy to keep them moving.

Scott was watching with interest as the parade passed him when the herder called to him. "Too late to try to count 'em now, sonny. You ought to have done that before you ordered the recount."

"Don't look as big as it did," Scott replied, frowning at the band and trying to look worried.

"It'll look smaller yet when the tail end of it goes through that chute this morning," the herder jeered.

"Well, I should worry," Scott retorted, "Dawson, Ramsey and Jed will be there to do the counting at ten o'clock. Are the others coming?"

"You bet, and crazy to get there. You won't have a very hard time counting yourself when this thing is over."

"Think not?" Scott replied teasingly, and he rode back toward the chute, leaving the herder cursing him for a conceited upstart who would soon get a proper calling down. He stopped in at the cabin to get his tally register, and then rode on down to the chute to see that all was in readiness there. It was still an hour and a half before the time set for the recount and Scott put in the time examining the fence on either side of the chute to make sure that there were no holes.

He had not gone far along the fence on the west side of the chute when he noticed something which aroused his curiosity. All the ground between two of the posts had been trampled up by sheep. Of course the sheep had been crowded pretty close up to the fence on both sides at the time of the counting, but this was different. There had been no rain since the sheep came in and the distinct, continuous trail could be plainly seen between the two posts. The ground was not trampled up that way between any of the other posts. Further examination showed that one of the posts was loose and that all wires had been cut at that point and renailed.

This was a new piece of evidence which Scott had almost missed. Evidently Dugan had been afraid that Scott would get back from that fake fire before he had time to get all the sheep through the chute and had opened up that hole in the fence to hurry things along. He had a pretty clear idea now of the plan the stockmen had used and just how they had worked it. He recognized now that Dawson was the brains of the whole ring and that it was his smooth craft which had made it work. No detail which could be foreseen had been overlooked.

There was a rattling of loose stones down the cañon trail and the supervisor appeared. He greeted Scott cordially. "You seem to have rounded up these fellows in pretty quick time," he remarked looking keenly at Scott.

"Yes," Scott replied modestly, "I was lucky enough to stumble onto it."

"I hope for your own sake and that of the service that you are not mistaken in your estimate. It takes a good deal of experience to estimate sheep accurately in the open."

"That is the reason I had Baxter do it for me," Scott replied.

"Oh," exclaimed Mr. Ramsey, evidently relieved, "he knows if any one does. When did you get him to do it?"

"The day after the sheep came in. I tried to count them and could not do it, but when I saw the bands in his district they looked so much smaller than mine that I asked him to come over and estimate them."

Just then Dawson rode up. "Well, Burton," he said when the first greetings were over, "don't you feel a little nervous?"

"Not in the least," Scott replied confidently.

"I never knew before," said the supervisor, "that it was possible to get sheep up those little cañons down there."

"It isn't," Scott said quietly, looking straight at Dawson. He thought that he detected a slight start, but he was not sure.

"Then how did they get in?" persisted the supervisor.

"Here is something here that looks rather suspicious," Scott said, leading the way to the trail through the fence.

Both Dawson and Ramsey examined it carefully. Scott called their attention to the loose post and the cut wires. He watched

Dawson closely but could not detect even a trace of worry in his face. The ranger was such a good actor that if Scott had not been positive of his guilt he would have begun to worry himself.

"That is where they went, all right," Dawson said, "probably ran them in at night."

Scott was dumfounded for a minute. He had never thought of that. Then an idea occurred to him. "Why didn't they take them through the chute if they did it at night?" Scott asked. He thought that he had him this time.

"Probably because they did it the night before the count and did not want you to see the tracks in the morning," Dawson answered.

Scott knew that such was not the case but it was a clever argument. He decided to keep his information till later. He had shown the supervisor how the sheep went in and that was all he wanted to do just then. Already they could hear the sheep approaching and before they reached the chute Jed joined them. He was sullen and had very little to say to any one. He avoided Scott altogether.

"We'll count them as they go out," Mr. Ramsey suggested. "You and I will do the counting, Jed."

"Yes, and I'll have some damages coming when we are through," Jed growled. "I'm not going to have my sheep driven all over the country for nothing."

The herders all looked so happy that the supervisor became worried. "Looks as though they had slipped you some way," he whispered to Scott.

Scott only smiled and replied, "We'll see."

The first band counted five under the permit, the second band sixteen under and the third twelve. The worried look deepened on the supervisor's face and Jed was growling louder and louder. Every one was rubbing it into Scott but he only grinned and waited.

The last sheep of the last band was counted and they had all come well within the limit. Mr. Ramsey turned to Scott and that hard, steely look was in his eye. Scott caught Dawson's wink at Jed.

"Where are your extras?" Ramsey asked severely.

"We'll go count them now," Scott said. He tried to speak calmly but a note of triumph stole into his voice in spite of himself. He noticed a decided look of dismay on Jed's face, but Dawson's showed no sign. Scott led his horse out of the brush.

"Where are you taking us now?" the supervisor asked coldly before he made a move to mount.

"Down where the sheep are," Scott retorted a little nettled, "they are not likely to bring them up here."

They all mounted and Scott led them up the trail in silence. He could have taken them directly along the bench at the edge of the cliff, but he preferred to go around by the ridge trail and keep them in suspense. He saw that the supervisor thought that he was bluffing. The farther they went along the ridge trail the more relieved Jed Clark looked, but when they turned short off the trail to the south his spirits dropped once more.

Scott rode straight for the cañon now. There was no one in sight and he did feel a little worried for a minute. What if they had moved those sheep in spite of Baxter? But he thought of Baxter and the three thousand sheep down at the foot of the cliff and knew that he had no reason to be nervous.

As they rode into the mouth of the cañon an astonished herder jumped from the improvised fence and stared at them wide eyed. Scott paid no attention to him, but led the others straight up to the fence. The bleating of hungry sheep had already reached them, but when Mr. Ramsey saw how many were packed inside the fence he whistled his amazement.

"We can make a little hole in this fence and count them as they go out," Scott explained. He still felt a little grouchy about Ramsey's attitude even when he looked at Jed's beaten face.

"Pretty clever scheme, Jed," the supervisor said patronizingly, "but Burton seems to have caught you at it."

Jed stared at Scott as though he would have liked to tear him to pieces, but maintained a sullen silence.

"How many are there in there?" Ramsey asked.

"About two thousand as nearly as I could judge," answered Baxter who had come up unnoticed.

Every one was too excited to even notice that he was a newcomer.

"Two thousand!" Mr. Ramsey exclaimed, "That is the most any one has ever tried to run in on me yet."

"That's not half of them," Scott said.

"What?" Ramsey cried. "Not half of them? Where are the others? Turn these out to get something to eat. You count them as they go out, Baxter."

Scott mounted and rode out of the cañon. The others followed closely. The silence of the other cañon was oppressive compared with the noise of the first one.

"Seem to have 'flued the coop,'" Dawson remarked.

Scott dismounted and tore a hole in the brush fence. He led the way down to the bottom of the cañon. "They're down there," he said pointing over the edge of the cliff.

The tracks leading into the narrow neck and the trampled shrubs along the edge of the cliff told the story only too plainly. Mr. Ramsey walked cautiously to the edge and looked over.

"Gosh," he exclaimed drawing back quickly. "That's an awful sight. How many were there?"

"Somewhere around three thousand," Scott replied; "I could not tell exactly."

"It was a clever scheme, Jed," Ramsey repeated, "but it did not work."

Jed was completely crushed. Scott felt sorry for him, little as he deserved it.

"It was a clever scheme, all right," Scott said, "but it was not Jed's."

"Who's was it, then?" Ramsey asked in astonishment.

Every one listened in strained silence. Baxter had joined the party contrary to orders to see the fun.

"Dawson's," Scott replied, looking straight at the ranger.

Every eye was turned on Dawson in amazement. Scott could not help but admire the man's magnificent nerve. The accusation must have come as a complete surprise to him, but not an eyelash quivered. He looked at Scott as though in surprised amusement.

"Mine?" he asked smiling. "I guess your success has gone to your head. How do you make that out?"

"I happen to know," Scott said looking Dawson calmly in the eye, "that you are Jed Clark's partner in the sheep business, that you recommended Heth as a patrolman on this district knowing him to be Dugan, a crook, and Jed's foreman, and that you planned this whole thing from start to finish."

There was a gasp of astonishment from every one except Dawson. Mr. Ramsey looked from Scott to Dawson in utter bewilderment.

"You are either going crazy or are a most magnificent liar," Dawson responded coldly. "You have made some statements here that you either have to prove or answer to me for."

A deadly hatred blazed for a moment in the ranger's face, but he quickly controlled it. He turned calmly to the supervisor. "I demand an investigation of this thing from start to finish."

The supervisor was clearly at a loss. The ranger's reputation during his past eight years of service was such that he could not believe that there was any possible foundation for the charges, and yet Scott had shown a remarkable skill in unraveling this matter so far and seemed confident of his charges.

"We shall certainly have to investigate it," he said. "You understand, of course, Burton, that you will be obliged to prove fully all the charges that you have made."

"I have the proof," Scott said quietly, "and can produce it whenever it is needed."

"Very well, I'll notify you when the hearing will be held. Jed, your permits are of course cancelled, but we'll have to let those sheep stay on here to keep them from starving till you have a chance to dispose of them. I want you to come down to the office with me, Dawson, to clear up some other matters there. You can stay here, Burton, and look after your district as usual. You have done a magnificent job in handling this problem so far and I congratulate you. Come on, fellows."

Mr. Ramsey was evidently anxious to get Jed and Dawson away from Scott. He, too, had caught the look of hatred and he was afraid it might blaze out any minute in open violence. He rode off toward the chute with the two stockmen and left Scott with Baxter who was eagerly waiting to hear an account of everything he had missed.

CHAPTER XV
THE MAN HUNT

"Gee," Baxter exclaimed when he heard the story. "You certainly are the lucky one. All that doing in your first week. It's more excitement than I have had in the past two years."

"It has been pretty good fun," Scott admitted, "but I suppose it will seem slow now that it is all over."

"Not if I know Jed and Dawson," Baxter exclaimed, "Jed is yellow and will never try a fair fight with you, but if I were you I would get a suit of mail armor for he is likely to try to shoot you in the back any time. Isn't old Dawson a smooth one, though? Here he has been doing that thing for three or four years and yet no one ever so much as suspected him of it. He will not say or do a thing until he knows which way this investigation is going. If he finds you have anything on him that he cannot get out of, then watch out. I did not know he was crooked but I know that he will not stop at anything to get what he wants."

"Sounds as though there might be some interest left in life yet," Scott laughed.

"If I were you I would come over to my shack and stay. You can work your district just as well from there and I can help you. It would not be so easy for them to pick on the two of us. One man does not stand much show alone; he has to sleep sometime."

"And let them think they had run me out," Scott exclaimed. "Nothing doing. I'm not afraid of them."

"There are times when a man has a right to be afraid," Baxter urged, "it isn't cowardice, it's only decent caution and common sense."

He was so earnest about it and so different from his usual daredevil self that Scott seriously considered his proposition. "Well, I can't run away now without any pretext, but if they make it too hot for me I'll consider it. If I have to run anywhere it will be to you."

"Good, I don't want to seem to croak but I expect to see you before long. Don't put off the running too long."

"By the way," Scott called just as he was starting back for the chute to see if the sheep were coming back all right to their allotted ranges, "have you had lunch? I forgot mine in the excitement and it is almost three o'clock."

"Forgot mine, too. Might as well eat together here before you go."

They brought their lunches from their saddle bags and continued the investigation discussion. Probably most of the people within fifty miles would be talking about it in the morning. They had scarcely swallowed the last sandwich when Scott noticed a distinct column of smoke rising over the ridge to the north.

"Hello," he exclaimed, "is that another of Jed's signal fires?"

Baxter took a long look at it. "No, that's no brush pile. There is no wind and yet the smoke seems to be pretty widely scattered. That's the trouble with this country; four days of sunshine and then fire will run in the needles. That cannot be far from the lookout station, but I suppose we better go up and have a look."

They mounted and rode up the slope together. As they approached the ridge it seemed very apparent that it was not a brush pile burning. The smoke was rising from a considerable area. From the ridge they could see it plainly. It was a ground fire on the lower slope just below the lookout station.

"Quickest way will be to ride to the lookout station and get a couple of shovels from the cache."

So they galloped up to the station and raided the tool cache. There was no one there. They grabbed the shovels and ran down the slope. The first person they saw was the lookout's wife, dressed in overalls and swinging a shovel like a ditch digger.

"Where is Benny?" Baxter called to her.

"He's working on the other end of it," she replied without turning from her work.

"Then I'm going over there," said Baxter with decision. "He's sent me out on many a dirty fire and I want the satisfaction of seeing him work on one himself. Don't know as I'll even help him unless it's pretty bad."

Only the needles on the surface were dry and a shovel full of the moist earth put out the fire wherever it reached it. Scott fell to work a little bit ahead of the woman and they progressed rapidly. It was only a few minutes till they met the lookout and Baxter and the fire was out.

"How did it start, Benny?" Baxter asked. "Throw a cigarette out the tower window?"

"Looks like it," Benny admitted. "No, some sheep herder did it. I happened to pick him up with the glasses away down by the cliffs, and I caught sight of him from time to time as he came up the valley, but I could not recognize him. Just about the time he reached the pass up there I found the smoke. Since then I have been too busy to think about him."

"He probably dropped a match," Scott suggested.

"It was a match all right, but I'll bet he did not drop it," Baxter commented. "Let's go see what we can find."

The emergency over, the lookout's wife had gone quietly back to her home work. The three men went down into the valley to investigate. They easily picked up the man's trail and found where it touched the edge of the burn. Sure enough, there was plenty of evidence to show that the match was not dropped carelessly. Pine needles had been carefully raked together in a long pile which had apparently been lighted in several places. No efforts had been made to efface the traces of the work.

"Just what I thought," Baxter exclaimed, straightening up with a frown.

"But why in thunder did he set the thing right under my nose?" asked Benny in an injured tone.

"Probably like the rest of us," Baxter laughed, "he wanted to see you work. No, that was just sheer bravado. That fire was set as a warning to show us what would happen if we pushed this sheep business and he wanted to put it where it would surely be seen."

"By the way," Benny asked with sudden interest, "how did the recount come out? I called up Dawson, but he was not home."

When he had heard the story he shook his head sagely. "If that is the way it stands I would not be surprised if that was what the fire was for. And I would not be surprised if there were some more of them in the next few days."

With this comforting piece of news Scott started back by the way of the bench to have a look at the sheep before he went home to supper. He found them all trailing back to the feeding grounds. The herders were in a sullen mood. Not that it made much difference to them who owned the sheep, but they felt the failure of the plan as a personal defeat and they took it out in hating the man who had frustrated the plan. They hinted darkly at what would happen to the district and its patrolman.

Their attitude furnished Scott with some food for thought. If these men who had no financial interests at stake felt as bitter as they did, he could well imagine the feelings of Dawson, Jed and Dugan. Two of them he knew to be unscrupulous and

Baxter had assured him that Dawson would be no better. He was beginning to think a little more seriously of Baxter's advice. It would be hard for one man to live alone and protect himself against three others for an indefinite time.

He had ridden so slowly that it was dusk when he turned Jed into the corral and went to the lonely cabin to prepare his supper. There was no evidence that any one had been there in his absence, but he felt uneasy. These men were not like the men he had known. If they would come out in the open and fight fairly with their fists he would not have thought twice about it, but the thought of being shot in the back with no chance at all seemed horrible. It was one thing to rush a man in the face of a loaded gun in the flush of excitement, and to feel hour after hour that the same gun may be aimed at you from behind a tree or from out of the darkness around the cabin. It was the unfairness of it all that oppressed him; the feeling that it was something over which he had no control.

Early in the evening the 'phone rang. He had already become so nervous that he jumped almost out of his skin at the sound. It was the supervisor.

"I have only a minute, Burton, and must talk fast. You made a beautiful clean up of that bunch to-day and from a few things I have found out since, I believe you are right about all the rest of it. Jed is crazy. He has loaded up on fire water and is telling every one what he is going to do to you and the whole service. I want you to keep out of his way. You are probably no match for him with a gun and moreover I do not want any fights if I can help it.

"I understand that the big reservoir on the upper plateau is about full. The snows are melting pretty fast now. I want you to start up there early to-morrow and watch it. When it reaches the twenty foot mark open the spillway; it will raise Cain if it overflows. Stop and tell Baxter to look after your district, but do not tell any one else where you are going. Do you understand?"

"I think so," Scott answered.

"I'll send for you when I want you for that investigation. So long. Take care of yourself."

Scott had forgotten his fears while the supervisor was talking, but with the click of the receiver the old loneliness came over him again. So Jed was on the war path and Ramsey thought there was danger. He recognized that his assignment to the reservoir was only an excuse to get him out of the way. He was glad of the excuse himself and wondered whether the sensible thing would not be to go to Baxter's for the night.

He had a hard time swallowing the idea of running away, even when he knew that it was the sensible thing to do. The cabin felt like a trap to him and he wandered out under the stars. He had a show there, no one could sneak up on him. He sat down on a log at the edge of the clearing and listened to the night noises as he had done so many times before. As the distant sounds floated up to him on the still night air and his trained ear caught the scurrying of tiny feet in the bushes about him, his confidence came back to him. He felt safe enough out there. It was just a matter of woodcraft now, and in that he was not afraid to put himself against any man. That would be a fair contest.

Far up along the ridge trail to the east a woman was running desperately. She was keeping to the shadow as much as possible and looking nervously back over her shoulder. Her breath was coming in gasps and it seemed as though she must give up, but she staggered on doggedly. The yapping of the coyotes and the lurking shadows of the forest trail seemed to have no horrors for her. They were overshadowed by another horror far more terrible. Her face wore a look of dread, but it was not the dread of the dangers of the night. She did not give a thought to her own safety. She was running a race with death and her only thought was that she might be too late.

She turned down the little trail to the patrolman's cabin and made one more desperate effort. Her strength was failing but the sight of the light in the cabin seemed to buoy her up and lend wings to her feet. There was yet time. She staggered uncertainly to the open door of the cabin. There was no one there. The disappointment was too much for her and she sank to the step with a sob.

To Scott, sitting quietly in the shadow of the forest's edge, the sight of this disheveled woman gliding into the flood of light from the cabin door had appeared like a specter. He hesitated a moment, suspicious of every one, but at the sound of that heartbroken sob he forgot his own danger and hastened to her. He raised the limp form gently and recognized Mrs. Dawson.

She raised her tired eyes dully, but at the sight of Scott she started up with unexpected strength.

"Oh, Mr. Burton," she gasped, "you must get away from here at once. There are some men coming here to kill you to-night and you must get away before they come."

"How do you know this?" Scott asked kindly, trying to help the exhausted woman to a chair in the cabin.

"No, no, not in there," she exclaimed in terror. "I must not be seen here. Why do you make me say how I know? It is bad enough to have to betray my husband without having to talk about it. But you saved Marie for me and I had to tell you. He will thank me for it some day. Now please go. They may come any minute."

"I must see you safely home first," Scott replied.

"No, no, they would kill us both. There is no danger for me in the woods alone. Oh, please go quickly and do not make me make this awful trip for nothing. Please go; you must." She began to sob again.

"I cannot tell you how much I appreciate this," Scott said earnestly. "They will not find me when they come. Good-by."

He stepped back into the outdoor shadows. "Will you promise me," the woman called after him in a broken voice, "not to shoot them when they come? I know I have no right to ask it, but won't you promise?"

"I don't even carry a gun," Scott assured her.

With a little gasp of thankfulness the woman disappeared into the shadows of the trail.

Scott retreated to his station on the edge of the forest and listened. There were a few faint clicks from the rolling pebbles on the trail and all was still once more. Scott had thought his position was bad enough but it seemed easy when compared with the dilemma of that poor woman, who had felt herself forced to betray her husband to keep him from murder, and to save the man who, she considered, had saved her child. He little thought when he picked the child up on the trail that day that he was piling up such a store of gratitude. In fact he had never even considered that he had really rescued the child; he had simply carried her home.

He certainly felt grateful to Mrs. Dawson. It was not half as hard to wait for trouble when he knew definitely that it was coming as it was to sit around and wonder about it. He could act now. At first he thought that he would go at once to Baxter's, but he could not resist the temptation to stay and try to find out who the men were who were after him. He went quietly down to the corral, put the saddle and bridle on Jed, and led him out a quarter of a mile in the direction of Baxter's quarters. He left the horse there in a well-marked spot and stole cautiously back to his station near the cabin.

It was too dark to see his watch, but Scott judged that it must be pretty close to midnight. Once more he settled down to wait and listen but he knew what to expect now and was entirely free from the creepy feeling of uncertainty which had so worked on his nerves earlier in the night. After about an hour's vigil he thought he heard a faint sound far down the trail. He waited patiently but it was not repeated. That, however, was not significant for they would probably leave their horses at a safe distance and come the rest of the way more quietly on foot. He continued to listen intently.

In about half an hour his patience was rewarded. A twig snapped in the direction of the corral and a dark shadow crawled slowly toward the cabin. Scott sat as still as the tree against which he leaned. It made him shudder to think that he might have been in that cabin with that crawling shadow sneaking up on him. The man moved very cautiously and as silently as the death that he carried. He avoided the glare of the light from the doorway and edged around toward the side next to Scott. His progress was almost imperceptible now but he finally reached the wall. He listened intently for a moment and then raised himself cautiously to a level with the window. For one second he stood in the glare of the lamplight before he realized that there was no one within and then he ducked quickly below the sill. He was quick to recognize the disadvantage of being there in the light with a possible enemy in the dark woods behind him.

Short as the time had been Scott had recognized Dugan and had caught the gleam of light from something which glittered in his hand. It was hard to realize that he had slept with that man for three nights in that very cabin. He did not have long to think about it for Dugan had made certain there was no one in the shack and was retreating to the very patch of shade in which Scott was hiding. He used the same stealthy caution with which he had approached the cabin and seemed to Scott to be gliding toward him for all the world like a snake. There was the same dull reflection every time he advanced his right hand that Scott had noticed in the window. It looked as though they were certain to meet if Dugan held to his present course. Scott almost stopped breathing and braced himself for the encounter. If only the man would come within reach. Scott felt that he could handle Dugan if he could only get hold of him before there was time to shoot.

Steadily the shadow advanced. Only eight feet separated him from the man in the forest when he turned slowly toward the cabin once more and settled down to watch. Scott could not have missed him, as poor a shot as he was, but even now he was glad that he was not armed. The idea of shooting a man in the back even when that man was waiting to do the same thing to him was repulsive to him.

Almost side by side the two men sat and watched in absolute silence. Scott had been still for an hour before he came without suffering the slightest inconvenience, now he suffered agonies.

He wanted to sneeze. He itched all over and had an almost uncontrollable desire to scratch. His legs became cramped and he felt that he would have to move them or scream. And still Dugan waited patiently, toying silently with his revolver. Scott saw the ridiculous side of the situation as well as the danger and grinned as he planned what he would do when the day began to break.

Dugan seemed to realize that something was wrong. He rose slowly and walked cautiously back to the window. He was bolder now. His vigil had convinced him that there was no one around. He made a careful survey of the inside of the cabin and then walked boldly off in the direction of the corral.

Scott heaved a great sigh of relief, congratulated himself on his foresight in getting Jed out of the way and sneaked cautiously out to join him. Jed heard him coming and nickered loudly. Scott had no doubt that Dugan heard it, but it was too late now to do him any harm. He swung onto Jed's back with a feeling of perfect safety and cantered away to Baxter's.

Baxter was standing in the door of his cabin waiting for him. "I heard your horse a mile away," he called in cheerful greeting. "Put Jed in the corral and come tell me the story. I have been lying awake all night just to hear it."

CHAPTER XVI
AT THE RESERVOIR

Scott and Baxter lay awake far into the small hours of the morning discussing the events of the past evening. Baxter had been in the West long enough to have lost his aversion to a gun, if indeed he had ever had any, and could not understand Scott's scruples.

"If ever a man had need of gun," he exclaimed, "you have now. Here you are traipsing around the country with a bad man on your trail and not so much as a cap pistol in your belt. Why, man, if you'd had a gun there to-night you could have blown that skunk into kingdom come and ended all this rumpus."

"And thought about it all the rest of my life," Scott replied.

Baxter looked at him hopelessly and gave it up. "Well, you ought to be pretty safe up there at the dam if they don't know you are there. Ramsey is evidently looking out for you down there and I'll keep a weather eye on the pass here. Let's go to sleep so that you can get away from here in the morning before anybody sees you."

The nerves of youth are easily settled and Scott was soon sleeping as peacefully as though nothing had happened. At his first snore Baxter raised up cautiously and crawled out of bed. He slipped on his clothes and took his seat at the open doorway with his revolver lying within easy reach. "Let that devil come snooping around here," he muttered, "and I'll see how my scruples work on him."

At the first streak of day the faithful guardian arose and quietly prepared breakfast. "Come out of it, Burton, and throw some of this into you," he called to Scott when all was ready.

"Why didn't you call me earlier?" Scott complained.

"Because I had not been out dodging bullets all night and did not need the sleep."

"How about grub up there at the dam?" Scott asked. "I don't know anything about the place and never thought about provisions last night."

"Strange, not having anything else to think about," Baxter commented sarcastically. "Better take along a few things from here to make sure, but the cabin up there is usually pretty well stocked, I think. If you are ready we better be going; we are not so likely to meet any one on the trail now."

He threw such perishable provisions as he happened to have into a bag and started for the corral. Scott saw him pick his revolver up from the bench by the door and stick it into his holster.

It was just light enough to see when they started up the trail which led over the pass. They were nearly to the place where they were fighting the fire the day before when Baxter turned from the trail into the heavier timber.

"What's the big scare now," Scott asked looking curiously around.

"May not be anything in it," Baxter replied, "but old Benny up there in the lookout tower has eyes like a hawk. If he sees anything moving within fifty miles he hauls out those old field glasses and identifies it. He might recognize you and spread the news all over the country. He is all right and would not tell any one if he knew why you were going, but he doesn't know and has nothing to do but talk gossip over the 'phone."

So they stuck to the hillside in spite of the rough going and managed to keep out of Benny's sight.

"Now you are all right," Baxter assured him. "This trail is not very good but you can follow it easy enough and it will lead you straight to the dam. There is not supposed to be any one up that way, but if you should see any one duck."

"I suppose there is a telephone up there?" Scott asked.

"Yes, and you better listen in on every call you hear, because some of us may want to warn you, but don't talk unless you are sure who it is. They might try to locate you that way."

"Well, so long," Scott said, "I certainly appreciate what you have done for me."

"Haven't had a chance yet," Baxter replied cheerfully, "but I am praying for the opportunity. Don't you think you better take my gun? I have another at the cabin."

"No," Scott laughed, "I might shoot myself. So long."

Once more he was alone with his thoughts, taking to the hills like a hunted animal and not knowing who might be on his trail or where. At least he felt certain that no enemies were ahead of him and he did not fear those who followed as long as he was in the open. He was going into a new country and that always pleased him. The thought of his dangers was soon wiped out by the wildness and ruggedness of the mountains around him.

This trail was little more than a cow track and he lost sight of it several times, but Jed followed it as easily as a hound no matter how vague it seemed to Scott. If this was the only trail to the dam he thought the supervisor had picked a very good hiding place for him. Here and there the mountains receded enough to make a fairly respectable valley, but for the most part they crowded in pretty close and left little more than a narrow cañon. There were traces of a dry stream bed in the bottom of it and Scott guessed that it was the spillway for the dam in time of flood. He noticed that if there should be much of a run-off there would be scant room for the trail.

After two hours of steady climbing Jed emerged into a small flat, grassy and an ideal meadow. At the upper end of the flat was a heavy mason work wall, twenty feet high in the middle and stretching clear across from slope to slope. Back of it was a great amphitheater surrounded by mountain peaks. It was a magnificent picture and Scott sat for a few minutes drinking it in. The grandeur of it awed him a little, but it had a wonderful, mysterious beauty that fascinated him. He had often read of the eagle's eyrie on the mountain peaks and now he felt that he had found it. The prospect of a week in that little cabin on the end of the dam would have been an unadulterated joy to him if it had not been for the silent hunter on the slopes below.

"Well, Jed, old boy, they were mighty considerate of you, anyway. I don't know what there is in that cabin but if it is half as well stocked as this meadow I'll be satisfied."

He threw the saddle and bridle on the ground in one corner of the meadow near the end of the dam and turned Jed loose to graze. A tiny stream trickled through the dam, in one place, filling a little basin in the sod of the meadow. Jed drank long and deep and seemed perfectly contented with his surroundings. There was no danger of his wandering off even if he had not been so faithfully attached to Scott. No dog could have thought more of its master.

An examination of the cabin showed ample supplies to withstand a long siege. The view back into the encircling mountains was superb and down through the cut of the cañon was a vista of hill and gorge that extended clear to the main valley miles away. There was eighteen feet of crystal clear water in the reservoir which was about twenty acres in extent. To a man from the lake-sprinkled section of New England it was a welcome sight. It was the most water he had seen in that semi-arid country.

The dam itself was a rather poorly constructed mason work affair and its safety was a matter of anxiety every spring to the ranchers who lived in the valley below. Since it had come into the hands of the Service, a man had been stationed there whenever the melting of the snows in the surrounding mountains threatened an overflow. Scott could not imagine a more pleasant job under normal conditions. He even felt that he could enjoy it now for he felt very little fear of not being able to take care of himself in such a place.

He marked the height of the water so that he could note its progress and went back into the cabin to fix it up for his occupancy. It was a cozy little place but Scott had not been in there long when he began to feel uneasy. The same old feeling of being trapped was stealing over him once more. He kept going to the door to peer down the cañon, and was constantly glancing at the window, half expecting to see Dugan's leering face and that glittering something in his hand. He tried his best to forget it and busy himself with the work in hand, but he could not do it. A few minutes in the open restored his nerve perfectly, but it began slipping again as soon as he returned to the cabin.

Scott hated to give in to these fears which he felt were almost entirely unwarranted, but he was forced to recognize that it would be out of the question for him to stay in the cabin. He would go crazy in there. It was a new sensation for a man who had always prided himself on not having any nerves, and just because it was new it was harder to bear.

"It's no use," Scott admitted to himself after struggling for an hour to stick it out. "I might as well own up to being a coward and act accordingly."

He went outside and looked for a good place to camp. There was no tent in the outfit but he did not need one. It seldom rained and if it should the cabin was there for shelter. He selected a little flat bench on the side of the cañon, near the cabin and slightly above it. It was backed by steep, overhanging rocks and could be approached only from the direction of the cabin. He could overlook the trail up the cañon but was protected from view by a thin screen of aspens.

He soon had a cozy little nest rigged up there and felt all his old assurance returning. The house was the handicap; here in the open he felt on an even footing with every man. The telephone was his problem now. He was supposed to listen for messages from below and yet he felt that he could not even listen intelligently cooped up there in the cabin corner with that 'phone where he could not even see out of the door or window.

A brilliant idea occurred to him. Why not move the 'phone up to the camp? There were tools for repairing the telephone line in all the cabins; he had everything that he needed. In an hour he had moved the instrument to the trunk of a little tree beside his camp and had reconnected it by extension wires. He ran his ground wire down into the water of the reservoir. He remembered his experience in trying to hold up a receiver for two or three hours and made a crude wire sling to hold it. Thus equipped like a telephone central he could listen indefinitely without inconvenience.

His new home satisfactorily furnished and equipped with all the modern conveniences, he set out to make a more comprehensive examination of the reservoir. There were a number of small streams running into it. During the heat of the day when the sun shone warm on the ice-capped peaks and melted the drifting snow in the deep packed cañons these streams delivered a considerable volume of water, but in the cool of the night they shrunk to a mere trickle, some of them ceasing to flow altogether.

Scott followed one of the larger ones away back and up to its hidden sources. He found side cañons packed with snow to the very rims and out of the bottom of each there trickled a tiny stream of ice cold water. In other places there were miniature glaciers thrusting their icy beaks out into the main cañon and melting as they advanced. The snow in the open was pretty well gone and there seemed to be little danger of a flood from those frozen reservoirs hidden so effectually from the direct rays of the sun.

There was only one great danger. Rain!

A heavy rainstorm on those barren peaks would inevitably mean an overwhelming flood. Most of the watershed was bare rock and there was very little vegetation to hold the rush of the assembled waters from the smooth worn channels of the ancient streams. Nor were there any pools or backwaters to delay the floods; nearly all were straight, narrow chutes leading to the reservoir below.

"One good thunder storm like we have at home," Scott thought, "would spill the water over the top of that dam before a fellow had a chance to open the flood gates; but they don't have them here, it just snows summer and winter." And so it did as a rule. Only a storm on an exceptionally warm day would produce rain at that altitude.

He climbed one of the lower peaks and there, perched on a block of old volcanic rock, he had the whole country laid out before him. The group of old Benny's lookout, which had seemed so high on the ridge above the valley cliffs, lay far below him. He could see the line of the cliffs and the fringe of trees along the stream in the main valley. A jutting rock was all that cut off the view of the town. The reservoir looked like a toy lake on the stage. There was quite a breeze up there on the rocks, but not a ripple marred the reflections on the surface of the pond. He could even see Jed feeding peacefully in the little meadow which appeared like a splotch of bright green paint spilled in the middle of an otherwise sombre picture. There was no limit to the view.

He searched all those miles of country within his vision for another moving object; there was none to be seen. He heaved a little sigh of relief and wondered when the time would come that he would be freed from the anxiety of watching for that pursuing shadow. It had been haunting him less than twenty-four hours, but they seemed to him like an eternity.

However, the worry had not yet affected his appetite and he started for the camp. He had climbed farther than he had realized. It took almost an hour of steady climbing to get down to the reservoir. He approached the camp cautiously but there was no trace of any one having been there and a nicker of welcome from the meadow told him that all was well with Jed. He ate his supper in comfort, put on his improvised head gear, and settled back against a mossy rock to listen to the gossip of the evening.

He watched the shadows chase the retreating sunlight up the eastern peaks and saw those shadows slowly deepen into darkness as the short twilight faded and disappeared. The world had gone to sleep and there came to his ear on the hushed night air the tinkling trickle of the little mountain streams and the plash of the water dripping through the dam. Suddenly the tips of the western peaks glowed white and the shadows came slowly down before the silver rays of the rising moon.

And not a word from the telephone. Either the people were unusually silent to-night or he had made some mistake in reconnecting his instrument. He was half dozing now, gazing dreamily at the moon herself balanced on the rim of the eastern peaks when he heard a faint click. It might have been the click of a receiver on the line or it might have been the cocking of a revolver.

Scott was wide awake now, as wide awake as he had ever been in all his life. He had been asleep and had that dreaded shadow stolen on him unawares, or was it only the telephone line? He had been too nearly asleep to know. For the next few minutes he sat with every sense alert and nerves on edge while he searched every shadow with anxious eye and listened in vain for the slightest suspicious sound. With a second slight click in the receiver he relaxed with a gasp of relief that could have been heard at the other end of the line if he had been anywhere near the transmitter.

It was another of those silent calls such as he had intercepted once before. He would have sworn that there were two men on that line now waiting to see if they had a clear field.

"Benson?" Scott recognized Dawson's voice. Benson was the grouchy clerk in the supervisor's office. So he belonged to the ring! Scott was glad of it; he had never liked the man but this was the first evidence that he had discovered against him.

"Well?" came the answer after a pause.

"Where did they assign the boob?"

"To watch the dam. Tried to tell you last night."

"Dugan and I were calling on him then."

"Going up?"

"To-morrow."

"Shoot one for me."

Two soft clicks and all was still.

So Mr. Dawson was coming to call in the morning. Well, Scott was glad to know it. Moreover, it made him feel that he was fairly safe from any visitors before that time. With this assurance he rolled in his blanket and went to sleep.

CHAPTER XVII
AN ATTEMPT AT BRIBERY

Scott awoke in the morning with a feeling of expectancy like a boy who has promised himself when he went to sleep that he would go fishing at four o'clock. He lay there drowsily for a moment watching the western peaks catch fire from the rays of the rising sun, and wondering vaguely what it was that he was going to do. His eyes rested for an instant on the telephone and he sat up with a jerk, awake to the situation.

He looked cautiously out over the dam and the cañon trail. It was not likely that Dawson would come so early in the morning. He did not know that Scott knew anything of his attempt to shoot him at the cabin and had no reason to believe that he would be expected at the dam. So there was no reason why he should come so early, but Scott intended to be prepared for him. He bridled Jed and led him over to the side of the meadow farthest from the trail and tied him back of a large clump of willows. He hid the saddle in a thicket near the trail.

He cooked his breakfast in the open with the receiver to his ear for he suspected that Baxter was on the lookout down below and might try to warn him. He was not nervous and excited as he had been that night at his own cabin, because he knew what was coming and felt prepared for it. Moreover, it was daylight and he was located so that he could see the only road of approach for some distance. There was no chance for an unexpected shot from an unseen foe.

It would have been easy enough to sneak back into the hills. He could elude an army up there among those crags where he had climbed the day before. But what good would it do? He could not wipe out the traces of his presence at the dam, he could not even make it appear that he had finished his business and left. He had made but a one way trail in the cañon and it would be an easy matter to find Jed even if he was hidden from sight.

No, there was nothing to gain by taking to the hills. He had been hunted long enough. He would stay and fight it out. He realized that being unarmed he would be at a tremendous disadvantage, but he thought he could manage it if he had the chance to plan the meeting as he wanted it. It was a desperate chance, but after his past experience he felt that no chance would be too desperate to escape becoming a hunted creature again, uncertain what danger might be threatening him next. He planned just what he would do in every contingency he could think of and had worked out everything so nearly to his own satisfaction that he was not in the least rattled when the telephone rang his own call at his district headquarters. He answered it promptly.

"This is Baxter. Benny reported Dawson going your way at nine-thirty. Somebody must have spilled the beans. Are you ready for him?"

"Sure," Scott answered with even more confidence than he really felt.

"Good. Then go to it. So long."

Scott took off his head gear and laid it aside. He glanced at his watch. It was ten fifteen. His visitor ought to arrive about eleven-thirty or possibly a little earlier if he was in a hurry. Scott went carefully over his plans once more to see if he could think of anything that he had overlooked. Then he settled down to watch the trail.

He was not at all nervous. He was waiting for something definite; he knew what it was, where it was coming from, and approximately when it would arrive. Moreover, he felt prepared to meet it. There was the same tense feeling of expectancy that he had often experienced when he was waiting for the opening of a boxing match, but no nervous shivers and no trace of fear.

It was a beautiful day. There were a few small clouds high up and moving slowly that cast a patch of shadow here and there on the broad landscape, but for the most part the sun shone brightly. A strange day Scott thought for a man to start out to commit a murder. Murders had always been associated with storms in the books he had read, and it was hard for him to think seriously of it on such a day as this. As the sun rose higher the little streamlets on the other side of the reservoir began to increase in volume and babble a little louder. All seemed peaceful. There was no place in that valley for strife and violence; and yet he knew that every tick of the watch was bringing it nearer.

His eye followed the shadow of a cloud slowly up the cañon slope till it disappeared over the ridge. When he looked back at the trail there was a horseman in full view. It did not startle him; it was what he had been waiting for, and he had a feeling of real satisfaction when he recognized Dawson. It would take him ten minutes more to arrive and he could watch him for at least half of that time.

Dawson did not act like a man who was bent on murder, at least he did not act as Dugan had that night at the cabin, and that was the only real experience that Scott had had. He was riding along the middle of the trail as he had always ridden about his work, with no pretense at secrecy and no attempt at silence. On he came in broad daylight as openly as he would have ridden to a wedding. Already the clatter of his horse's iron-clad hoofs on the loose stones of the trail was plainly audible. Surely this man could be on no business of which he was ashamed.

When horse and rider disappeared in a willow thicket just beyond the lower end of the pasture Scott stepped quickly from his hiding place and took up his position behind a large rock which lay near the cabin and close beside the trail. He had no idea of avoiding this man, but he wanted to pick his own meeting place and have him within easy reach of his hand when he was discovered. Only in that way could he hope to have a fair chance with that revolver. He could see through a screen of brushes beside the rock and watch his visitor after he entered the meadow.

The horse stopped on the edge of the meadow and breathed in the smell of the lush grass with deep noisy breaths through wide distended nostrils. It was something to which he was little accustomed. The delay seemed to suit the master's mood. He sat idly in his saddle, apparently fascinated as Scott had been by the grandeur and peaceful beauty of the scene.

His eyes were not searching the cabin and the immediate vicinity for a hunted man. He was gazing dreamily back into those encircling peaks and rugged, picturesque cañons. Even at that distance Scott could see a pensive sadness in his expression. Any one who had ever had business dealings with him in the past would have been amazed to know that at that moment he would have been willing to trade all his ill gotten gains to be freed from the burden of his crimes and be able to roam those mountains once again as an honest man. He loved those barren peaks and rocky cañons. He knew every rock and tree and bunch of grass in all that countryside. They had been his life. And now he realized too late that he had risked and maybe lost it all for the sake of something he did not need.

He sat still so long that even his horse stopped cropping the luscious grass and turned his head to look at him inquiringly. Scott, too, was becoming uneasy. Could he have anything to fear from a man who gazed at the beauty of the hills like that?

It did not seem possible, but he could not afford to take any chances and determined to be on his guard just as he had planned.

Dawson seemed to be coming slowly to himself. He had been dreaming of what might have been. He was more of a sentimentalist than even his friends had ever realized but was also somewhat of a philosopher. What was gone was gone and he must make the best of what was left. Nor would he let any one interfere with his success. The dreamy pensive look was gone now and in its place was the gleam of a hard determination which had made men say that when Dawson wanted anything bad enough he always got it.

He looked sharply about him, shook himself together and rode straight across the meadow to the foot of the dam. He dismounted and climbed the foot trail which led up past the end of the cabin. Scott tried to forget the man he had seen a moment before. He thought only of the look of hatred that this man had given him when he had accused him by the valley cliffs, and that he was the self-confessed companion of Dugan on that horrible night visit to the cabin. He thought of that man and waited for him with every sense alive to the danger of the situation, and prepared for immediate action.

Dawson came on straight up the trail and headed for the cabin without the slightest hesitation. Whatever might be his own intentions he did not seem to have the slightest misgiving about the other fellow's. When he passed the big rock Scott stepped quickly into the trail immediately behind him.

"Looking for me?" he asked sharply. He was ready to spring upon the man at the first sign of a hostile move.

Dawson turned quickly. "So there you are," he exclaimed. "Yes, I was looking for you and I have had the deuce of a time finding you." He seemed perfectly at ease and not in the least taken back by Scott's sudden appearance.

"I was transferred up here yesterday morning," Scott explained. He thought maybe Dawson's curiosity to know what had become of him the night before that would show itself, but it had no effect.

"So I found out later," he admitted so frankly that Scott wondered whether he really could have been with Dugan, or whether he could possibly have mistaken the voice on the 'phone the night before.

"Let's sit down, I have a lot of things I want to talk over with you," and without waiting for an answer he sat down on the ground with his back against the great rock and his face toward the rugged mountain peaks. Scott accepted the invitation but carefully selected a position where he would still be within easy reach of Dawson's pistol arm.

"I could sit here for a week and look at that view," Dawson said wistfully, and the dreamy look was stealing into his face again, "but that's not what I came for," he added, bracing himself up quickly. "That was a clever job you did in ferreting out those extra sheep. I don't know where in the thunder you got onto all that stuff, but you seemed to be able to produce the goods. However, I think you overreached yourself a little and made some statements which you can never prove."

"I think I was careful not to say anything which was not true," Scott replied cautiously.

"Possibly you were, but stating a truth is one thing and proving it is often something different."

"I think that I can prove them," Scott said quietly.

"Well, I doubt it. Now let's admit for the sake of the argument that all the statements you made were true, excepting, of course, your ability to prove them. You proved that there were more sheep than there were permits, but you did not prove how they got on the forest. Your inference is that Dugan let them through that hole in the fence while he was counting the others through the chute. But you can't prove it. Maybe he put them all through the fence without counting them, but there was no one there to see it. Your evidence is entirely circumstantial and would not stand in any court.

"You said that I was a partner of Jed's and directed all the scullduggery. That is hardly likely, but suppose that it were true. You can't prove it. You think that I recommended Dugan's appointment, but I didn't. He was assigned to us by the district office and nobody on the forest had anything to say about it. You may say that I had the district office appoint him, but you can't prove it. There is no proof that I am Jed Clark's partner. It does not exist. You may know—it beats me how you found it out if you do, but you may know—that I hold a mortgage on Jed's ranch. Even that would be hard to prove for the mortgage is not recorded. But a mortgage is no proof of partnership or even of complicity.

"You have woven a web of circumstantial evidence around me that looks bad. It would not stand in a court of law for a minute, but it will look nasty and will ruin my reputation. It will not do you any good to lose out in the law suit. In fact it may harm you with a lot of people because it will look as though you were trying to slip something over on me to push your own advancement. Of course you want to make good. You want to clean up this crooked business and make the best showing that you can. But I do not believe that you want to ruin a man for nothing."

"You are perfectly safe in thinking that," Scott said. He thought that Dawson was trying to pump him to see what information he really had. Yet, the ranger was not asking many questions or giving him much chance to talk. He could not make out just what the game was. It was too deep for him.

"I thought so," Dawson said resuming his story. "When I first came to this country ten years ago I had lived on the prairies all my life and hated them. They were so flat that you could look till your eyes ached and not see anything. The wind blew from one week's end to the next and there was no getting away from it. I fell in love with these old mountains as soon as I laid eyes on them and I would have taken any job which would have given me a chance to be in them and live. This forest service job was better than that. It gave me a home in the heart of the mountains, a good living and a little more. I had a good business head and I invested my savings in sheep. I was successful and amassed a small capital. I could have left the service and made a fortune in sheep, but I liked the mountains too well to leave them for wealth. I accumulated considerable property more as mental exercise than anything else. I had no use for the money and would not leave the mountains and this outdoor life for any amount of wealth.

"So you see what my life here and my reputation mean to me and how little I care for the money I have made. You on the other hand are a young man, probably seeking your fortune in any field that shows the best chances. There is big money in sheep for the man who will devote his life to it.

"I have tried to show you what this life means to me. I think I have shown you how utterly impossible it would be for you to prove your case. You will only succeed in ruining me without helping either yourself or the service."

"I can't agree with you," Scott said, "because I think that I can prove all those things." The man talked so frankly and pled so earnestly that it was hard to believe him utterly false. Scott began reviewing his evidence to see if it was really as purely circumstantial as Dawson had said it was.

Dawson looked at him keenly and thought that he was wavering. "Drop this impossible charge against me," he said suddenly, "and all my accumulations of the past ten years are yours."

So that was his game? All this smooth story was but the craftily laid background for the offering of a bribe. He was taking the last desperate chance of buying himself out of a hole which he knew to be otherwise hopeless.

Scott's growing sympathy turned instantly to disgust. "You can't bribe me," he sneered contemptuously, "any more than your hired cutthroat could bluff me."

The change in Dawson was instantaneous. The look of sentimental pleading was gone and his eyes flamed with malignant hatred. So sudden and violent was his fury that Scott involuntarily recoiled before it. Dawson sprang to his feet, out of reach, and drew his revolver.

"Fool," he hissed between his clenched teeth, "you are too good for this world."

The neighing of a horse in the meadow below stayed his hand for an instant. Furious as he was he realized that he would gain nothing if he freed himself from the charge of being a crook only to be branded as a murderer. He cast a hurried glance toward the meadow.

In that instant Scott hurled himself upon him. He struck up the revolver with his left hand and followed through to Dawson's chin with his right. The report of the revolver dazed him and the sight of the barrel pointed at his breast had almost made him sick, but he struck that blow with all the desperation of a dying man backed by years of training. Dawson sank down without a sound.

Scott stood dazed for a second hardly knowing what had happened. He half thought that he had been shot. The sight of the smoking revolver still grasped in Dawson's fingers brought him to his senses with a jerk. He flung himself upon the gun and snatched it from the unresisting hand. He took off Dawson's belt, turned him over on his face, and bound his wrists together with the belt. He slipped the holster onto his own belt and dropped the pistol into it. One such experience was enough. He knew now how helpless an unarmed man was. He hated a gun but he never wanted to be taken at such a disadvantage again. The vision of the muzzle of that "forty-five" would always be with him if he lived to be a thousand.

The hot sun was blazing down on the unconscious man and Scott dragged him into the shade of the aspens beside the camp. He was trembling from head to foot and now that the excitement was over he felt so weak that he was glad to sit down in the shade and try to think.

He looked out once more across the peaceful waters of the reservoir at those stately guardian peaks and shuddered to think how near he had been a few minutes before to losing his beautiful world forever.

CHAPTER XVIII
A STORM AND A MADMAN

Scott sat for some minutes gazing absently at the rugged mountains. He felt tired and his mind wandered listlessly from one vague something to another, none of them connected with the present situation. The peace and quiet of his surroundings began to soak into him and a lassitude crept over him. He had been under a much greater nervous strain than he had realized and the reaction made him sleepy. He wanted to curl up right where he was and sleep. He had no interest in anything else. His heavy eyes closed wearily and he sank down beside the still unconscious man.

Scott dreamed that he was lying on the battlefield with other wounded and dying men groaning all around him. The ambulance corps picked him up and carried him far back of the lines to a peaceful little French village surrounded by high mountains and put him in a little cabin beside a lake. He could hear the babbling of many small streams and the gentle lapping of tiny waves on a pebbly shore. They were soothing, lulling sounds but woven through them he could still hear the groans of the dying. The cabin was becoming unbearably warm and oppressive. He writhed about on his burning couch until the discomfort awoke him.

The groaning continued and Scott sat up suddenly to find that Dawson had regained consciousness. His jaw was badly broken, and it was his moaning that Scott had heard in his dreams. The sun was shining directly on them both with a blistering heat unusual for that time of the year. Scott did not know how long he had been asleep but it must have been a long time. The sun had shifted to the western half of the sky, a warm breeze was ruffling the surface of the reservoir, and black clouds were peeping over the horizon. Dawson was half delirious from suffering and lack of water in the blazing sun. He was moaning constantly and talking incoherently. He did not seem to recognize Scott or to know where he was.

Scott picked up the suffering man as carefully as he could and carried him into the cabin. All his feeling against Dawson was gone now and he saw only a human being in agony. He reproached himself for going to sleep and leaving him in such a condition. He realized now how panic-stricken he must have been to bind the wrists of a crippled man when he himself was armed with the cripple's revolver. He removed the belt from Dawson's wrists and ran out to get some water from the reservoir. He poured some of it on the parched lips and the injured man swallowed eagerly though every movement of his mouth seemed to cause new agony. Scott bathed his fevered brow, gave him a little more water to drink and then bound up his jaw with his handkerchief. He wondered how he could get him home. There were two horses there now, but Jed was not well enough trained to be trusted with one end of a stretcher. A trailing pole stretcher on Dawson's horse would be too rough.

He decided that his best move would be to 'phone down to Baxter or Benny for help.

His anxiety to aid the suffering man had so completely occupied Scott's attention that he had not noticed what was going on outside. A sudden gust of wind forced his attention. He ran to the door. The little black clouds which were just peeping over the horizon a short time before had spread over half the sky. The heat was oppressive and a warm, sultry wind which was blowing half a gale seemed only to accentuate it. Angry little waves were beating on the shore now and the growing streams on the other side of the reservoir were beginning to roar ominously.

Scott ran down to the edge of the reservoir to look at the mark he had set on the dam the day before. The water had already risen a foot since he had noticed it that morning and he knew from the rush of waters in the cañons that it was rising now at an alarming rate. He glanced at his watch. It was five o'clock. Ordinarily the cool of the approaching evening had begun to tie up the springs of ice and snow in the hidden cañons before that time and the streams would be drying up, but to-day that hot wind was searching its way into every cranny of the rocks and melting the winter's store of ice at a tremendous rate. Nor would they cease to melt even with the setting of the sun as long as that wind continued. A warm rain on top of that was almost sure to be disastrous.

Even while Scott looked the last patch of blue was blotted from the sky and the little basin was thrown into semi-darkness. The swiftness of the onrushing storm was bewildering. He would 'phone Baxter for help to get Dawson out of there and then open the sluice gates without waiting for the level of the reservoir to reach the danger point. He feared that it would reach it all too quickly even with the sluice gates open.

Scott rushed up the bank to the little camp and grabbed the telephone. He gave Baxter's ring and waited what seemed an age. He tried three times without getting any answer. Baxter must be either out on the range or out of hearing of the 'phone. He tried Benny. Benny was always there.

"Hello," came the prompt answer.

"That you, Benny? This is—"

He was interrupted by a blinding flash followed instantly by a deafening explosion. The receiver was apparently wrenched from his hand and he stood dazed while the reverberations of the mighty report were hurled crashing from peak to peak. The storm was on them. He grasped the 'phone again desperately but the fuses were burned out and the line was dead.

The echoes of the first crash of thunder had not died away in the distant hills when the rain came down in torrents. A half hour of that and the reservoir would overflow even if the dam itself did not go out before that. The opening of the sluice gates was the only thing which he could do. He could not imagine those sluice gates taking care of the mad torrents which would soon be raging down the cañons from all those encircling barren peaks, but the storm might possibly cease as suddenly as it had begun.

Scott sprang to the gates and was already bending his back to the old-fashioned windlass when he remembered that Jed was on the other side of the meadow. Once he had opened those gates it would be impossible to get him across to the trail. He had to have Jed to get help for Dawson and carry the warning of the impending danger to the ranchers along the course that the flood would take if the dam should burst.

The rain continued to fall in a deluge which almost blinded him, but he managed to stagger across the meadow to the clump of willows where he had left Jed. He feared that the horse might have been frightened by the storm and run away. The booming of the thunder in those hollow cañons was enough to terrify either horse or man. But Jed had spent his life in the open. Thunder storms in the mountains were nothing new to him. Close in the lee of the bushes, with his tail to the storm, he was waiting patiently. He greeted Scott with a little nicker of recognition.

Scott jumped on to his slippery, wet back and rode across the darkening meadow toward the place where he had hidden the saddle. He put on the saddle while there was yet light and leaving Jed well up from the trail, he dashed once more for the sluice gates. In the trail at the foot of the dam he almost ran into a strange horse. The poor beast was saddled and bridled and steaming in the rain from hard riding. Its breath was coming in great gasps, its head hung down until its nose was almost on the ground, and its feet were spread wide, a sign of total exhaustion. Some one had ridden up that steep cañon trail at a killing pace.

"It must be Baxter," Scott thought as he ran past the heaving horse and made for the sluice gates. There was not enough daylight left to recognize objects at any distance, but almost continuous lightning flashes made things stand out momentarily with vivid distinctness. Scott was just rounding a clump of bushes not more than ten yards from the sluice gates, when one of these lurid flashes revealed a picture which brought him to a sudden halt with his heart in his mouth.

Seated on top of the sluice gates was not Baxter, but Jed Clark.

He was crazy with drink. He was holding a forty-five in either hand. After every flash of lightning he waved the revolvers wildly in the air and shouted his vengeance against the forest service, the government and all law in general. He seemed to revel in the wildness of the storm. He was raving mad.

Scott stood as one stunned. He was in the shadow of the bushes and Jed had not seen him. He knew that Jed had come up there with the original intention of getting him. Failing to find Scott his crazed brain had now hit on the still more devilish scheme of reeking his vengeance on the forest service by bringing about the destruction of the dam. None knew the country better than he. None knew better than he how impossible it would be for that old dam to withstand the flood which was gathering against it. Now utterly regardless of his own danger he was seated on the sluice gates of the very dam he was planning to destroy, recklessly chanting his vengeance in the face of the raging elements.

The whole thing seemed so fiendish, so utterly inhuman, that Scott stared helplessly for a moment in an agony of dismay. His first impulse was to rush the maniac, for the gates must be opened and that quickly. But he gave up the idea almost as soon as he conceived it. Jed was well known to be a dead shot, drunk or sober, and the experience of the morning had shown Scott how perfectly helpless he would be.

There was only one way out. Dawson's revolver. It had been in his way when he was ministering to Dawson's hurts and he had taken it off. He started for the cabin and it suddenly occurred to him that Jed would have gone there the first thing. He remembered the unrecorded mortgage and Jed's veiled threat at that night meeting below the chute. He trembled to think what he might find in the cabin. Shivering he groped his way across the room to the bed. He leaned over it and waited for the next flash of lightning. It came and the frozen look of horror in the wide staring eyes of the man before him made his blood run cold. He wanted to run from the cabin but Dawson grabbed him by the sleeve. He tried to tell Scott something but the mumbled words from the tightly bound jaws were lost in the raging of the storm.

Scott realized that Jed had been to the cabin. He apparently had not in his drunken search noticed Dawson, but the injured man, helpless as he was, had been dreading his return. When Scott leaned over him he had thought that it was Jed and felt that his time had come. He held onto Scott now until the next flash could show him pointing to the dam. "Jed," he tried to say between his closed teeth.

Scott understood. He leaned close to Dawson's ear and shouted above the booming of the storm, "I saw him. I'm going after him now."

He picked up the revolver from the table and started out of the cabin. The last of the daylight was gone now and the frequent flashes of blinding lightning were separated by short periods of Stygian darkness. The recurring echoes of one mighty crash of thunder never died away till there was another crash that seemed louder yet. The effect was cumulative. It was as though all the storms of the ages had been dumped into that little caldron in the midst of the mountain peaks.

If the ground had been more familiar it would have been an easy matter for Scott to have utilized the lightning flashes to locate the next patch of shelter and to have run to it in the ensuing darkness, but he had not been there long enough for that. The vivid flashes confused him and everything looked strange in the weird light. It did not matter how much noise he made for nothing would be heard above the storm but he had to keep under cover for the lightning made objects stand out with uncanny clearness.

He trembled to think what he was going to do. It seemed the irony of fate that he, who had always shunned the use of a revolver and shuddered at the thought of shooting a man even in the heat of action, should now be called upon to shoot a man in cold blood. But there was nothing else to do. The lives of women and children in the valley below hung on the chance of getting that maniac away from the sluice gates. Scott accepted the call of fate, closed his senses to his own feelings, and crept on with unwavering determination. His mind was made up. He would shoot this man as he would shoot a mad dog to save the lives of others.

He had made his way almost to the clump of bushes where he had first discovered Jed—he had to get close or he knew that he would miss—when a flash of lightning revealed another object crawling around that same clump of bushes. Surprised as he was he recognized it even in that brief flash. He recognized the cautious snake-like crawl, and that gleaming steel. It had been graven on his memory that evening at the cabin when he had sat in the shadow of the forest and watched that same snake-like object crawl toward his cabin window. He could recognize it instantly anywhere.

But what was Dugan doing there at this out-of-the-way dam in a raging storm, and crawling inch by inch with a gun in hand toward the man who had been his friend? Either he had not recognized Jed and thought that he was stalking Scott, or had some ulterior motive which Scott did not know anything about for disposing of Jed. It was probably the former. Scott noticed that Jed was no longer brandishing his guns and shouting curses in the teeth of the storm. A fit of sullen depression had apparently come over him and he was crouched in a heap so that it was difficult even to recognize him as a man, to say nothing of determining his identity.

Dugan evidently wanted to make sure. He could easily have picked the man off from where he was, but he wormed his way steadily nearer. He was beyond the last piece of cover now and was working his way across the narrow open space which separated him from the sluice gates of the dam.

The storm instead of abating seemed to be increasing in fury. Flash followed flash almost without cessation. The crashing of the thunder sounded like a barrage of hundreds of big guns. And through it all there sounded the rush of waters. There seemed to be but one inanimate object in the whole scene. Trees and rocks and mountain peaks seemed to be dancing in the fickle flashes of light. The man on the sluice gates only seemed motionless. Perhaps he had gone to sleep in that perilous position on those groaning sluice gates.

Scott watched with a curious fascination. It seemed to him that fate had thought better of her irony and was sending this special agent to relieve him of his odious task. He was perfectly willing to have it so. It was like a reprieve from a horrible sentence. It had but one disagreeable feature. It was so maddeningly slow. He dreaded lest he should hear the dam giving way almost any minute.

Dugan did not seem to be in any hurry. He wanted to make sure. He evidently doubted whether the motionless object on the sluice gates was his man. He was lying perfectly still now watching it. He did not want to risk a shot at a scarecrow and sound a warning. Convinced at last that he was mistaken he rose to his feet and took a step toward the sluice gates.

There was a spit of flame, the roar of a forty-five, accompanied by a mocking laugh from the motionless object on the sluice gates, and Dugan staggered. He was hard hit but he was not the man to go alone. He steadied himself. There were two more reports almost simultaneously and the flashes from the two revolvers almost met.

Jed pitched backwards into the deep boiling waters of the reservoir and Dugan sank silently beside the sluice gates. Fate worked it out without Scott's aid.

CHAPTER XIX
THE BURSTING OF THE DAM

There was no time to waste in mourning over the fate of the two outlaws. Scott's first duty was to the unsuspecting ranchers in the path of the coming flood. The waves were already washing over the top of the dam and the old sluice gates were groaning under the strain. The storm still raged in unabated fury. Everywhere there was running water. It was coming down the face of the rocky slopes in sheets and all the cañons were filled with boiling torrents. The roar of it sounded like a mighty accompaniment to the booming of the thunder.

Before the echoes of the pistol shots had been swallowed up in the other noises of the storm Scott sprang for the windlass, but he was too late. Jed Clark was dead but he had accomplished his crazy purpose. With a crash and rending of heavy timbers the sluice gates went out on the crest of the flood and carried a small portion of the dam with them. The whole structure trembled from end to end. Scott felt the mason work crumbling under his feet and the swirling waters grasping at his ankles. He scrambled desperately out of its clutches and rushed to the place where he had left Jed. He was gone, but a frightened snort from higher up the steep side of the cañon led him to where the terrified horse had climbed to the base of the perpendicular wall of rock and stood trembling, too frightened to move.

The one chance now was to beat out the flood. To reach the ranchers in the valley below before the wall of water which would come when the dam went out, and that could be only the matter of minutes now. It was a desperate chance, for the trail was steep and rough, and the rush of the waters would make it almost impassable in places.

Scott flung himself onto Jed's trembling back and turned him down the cañon trail. Another crash in the direction of the dam sent him plunging ahead, and once started a mad fright took possession of him. He ran like a fiend. Scott had learned much about riding since he had cleared the corral fence clinging to Jed's neck, but it required all his skill to stay in the saddle now. He had to close his eyes to protect them from the twigs which slashed his face, and once a jagged point of rock grazed his knee and almost threw him from the horse's back.

"It's up to you, Jed, old boy," Scott whispered in the horse's ear, "I can't help you any now."

The roar of the torrent was always with him. Now the trail dipped down to its very edge, into it once; now it climbed high on the side of the cañon and skirted a narrow ledge at the edge of a wall of rock. The hollow booming of the waters hinted of sickening depths within easy reach of a misplaced foot. It seemed marvelous to Scott that Jed could run at that breakneck speed on such rugged ground, but the horse had been born in the mountains, had raced over them all his life, and he never stumbled.

He was gaining on the flood. Already he had passed the crest of the wave from the shattered sluice gates. There was water in the stream, plenty of it, from the drainage below the dam, but it was not the raging torrent which it had been higher up. The storm was lessening now. A star or two were peeping through the rifts in the black clouds and the profiles of the mountains were beginning to loom in darker shadows. Scott recognized the ridge ahead where the lookout station was located. He had to turn to the left there and follow the valley instead of going up over the pass the way he had come. From there on the country was wholly new to him and he would have to trust entirely to Jed. He wondered whether he ought to try to stop at the station and get Benny to telephone the news.

A dull roar like the rumble of distant thunder shook the mountain and Scott knew that the dam had given way. There was no time to lose now. The rush of water from the sluice gates would be like a dribble compared with the mighty avalanche of water which would roar down the valley now. Moreover, Jed was not yet under control and he would do well if he could hold him in the valley trail, to say nothing of stopping at Benny's.

He began to talk soothingly to Jed and tried to steady him a little. As he approached the turn in the valley he made out a figure standing on the opposite edge of the stream. He recognized Benny and tried to stop, but Jed was not yet ready to listen to reason. Scott succeeded in turning him, probably because he did not want to cross the stream, but he could not stop him. He had no control over him at all.

"The dam is gone. Telephone," he shouted at the top of his voice as he rushed past. Either Benny did not understand or could do nothing for he stood there quietly on the edge of the stream and listened to the roar of the cañon.

The ground was more even here in the wider valley, and much easier going for the horse. He had already covered five miles at that terrific pace, and although it did not seem to be telling on his splendid physique it seemed impossible for any animal to keep that up for the remaining fifteen miles to the valley. Scott began to talk to him once more. It was the only influence to which the big horse had ever seemed susceptible. There was no longer the roar of the water in the cañon to frighten him. There were not the same deafening thunder crashes with their weird reverberations, the rending of the gates was fading from his memory. Gradually Scott could feel the straining effort lessening. He was still making splendid time, but he was running more smoothly and he turned back his ear to listen when Scott talked to him.

Four miles of that smooth running in the upper valley and then down the steep trail to the main valley in which the town was located. The trail came out to the plain near the home of the last rancher whom Scott had gone to see about the free use permits. It was here that the strange procession had ended that day. As Jed shot out of the cañon into the open a man's form darkened the lighted doorway. Evidently he had heard the clatter of the rapidly approaching hoofs on the rocky trail.

Scott slowed down and shouted, "The dam has burst. You better beat it. Telephone the others."

He loosened the rein and Jed sped on. The figure disappeared instantly and looking back over his shoulder Scott could see the lights bobbing about the house. It was a warning of disaster to those people and they did not hesitate. It meant the destruction of their homes and all of their possessions which they could not move to the higher ground along the base of the valley cliffs.

At each of the other houses he had to stop and shout to get the people out. They had had no warning. The whole telephone system had been disabled by the storm. The message delivered, there was no delay, no stopping to get an explanation. The men sprang silently back to the houses and wasted none of the precious moments which were left them. They had been living in dread of just this thing for years and now it had come. They had been fearing it too long to be in any doubt as to what to do now.

All along behind Scott men were fleeing from their homes as from a pestilence with their families and most valuable possessions in wagons and driving their stock before them. There was many a backward glance at the homes which would probably be ruined when they saw them again.

After each stop Scott watched Jed anxiously to see if he was in distress but each time the noble animal took up his task willingly and was soon back in his swinging run which sent the miles flying behind him.

There was nothing ahead of him now but the town only two miles away, and Jed was pounding over the level plain with hoof beats as regular as the ticking of a watch. The town was all aglow with lights and the people were busy with their everyday affairs, ignorant of the impending danger.

Scott shouted his warning to every man he saw as he galloped up the main street and left a trail of confusion behind him. By the time he reached the hotel the news was ahead of him. The supervisor ran out of the hotel to meet him. A cowboy on a fresh horse galloped away with the warning for the people below the town.

Scott threw himself from the saddle without counting on the effect of the long, hard ride. His knees doubled under him like the blades of a jackknife and sent him sprawling in the street. A dozen eager hands helped him to his feet. He wriggled from them and staggered over to examine Jed. The big black was tired and showed it. His long barrel was heaving like a pair of bellows and his nostrils were distended to big red circles, but he was holding his head well up and he had his legs well under him. Scott threw his arms around the horse's neck and hugged him there before them all.

"Where did you come from?" Mr. Ramsey asked.

"Clear from the dam," Scott said proudly, "and he ran every step of the way."

"Didn't run down that cañon trail from the dam, did he?" one of the men grinned.

"You bet he did," Scott said. "He was running away with me then; I did not get control of him till we passed the lookout station."

It was perfectly natural in this country of horsemen that the first interest should have been in the performance of the horse. There was no actual danger there at the town. The valley was so wide and level at this point and it was so far from the cañon that at the very worst there would be only a few inches of water in the streets and a few flooded cellars. The storekeepers were busy getting their supplies from the cellars and off the main floors on to the shelves, but they had all the help they could use and there were plenty of people left over with nothing to do but watch and wait and talk.

Mr. Ramsey and Scott took Jed around to McGoorty's stable and gave him the best rub down that a horse ever had.

"When did the dam go out?" Mr. Ramsey asked.

"I don't know what time it was," Scott said, "but it was just before I turned the corner below the lookout station."

"Did you see all the settlers?"

"Yes, every one from Bronson's to town and they did not lose any time in getting started."

"How did it happen?" Mr. Ramsey asked quietly.

Scott discovered a note of censure in his voice and knew that he was expected to give an account of himself.

"It's a long story," he replied thoughtfully. "Dawson, Jed Clark, Dugan, myself and the worst thunder storm I have ever seen were all more or less responsible, I think."

At the mention of those names, Mr. Ramsey gave a start. "I wonder how those men found out you were up there?"

"Your clerk, Benson, told them."

"How do you know that?" the supervisor asked sharply.

"I heard Dawson ask him over the telephone and he answered that he had tried to get the information to him for some time but could not locate him."

The hard steely look came suddenly into the supervisor's eyes. "That accounts for the way that a lot of information has been leaking out of my office," he remarked coldly.

"By the way," Scott said, "Dawson is lying up in that little cabin at the dam with a broken jaw. He is in pretty bad shape and some one ought to go after him."

"I don't suppose you know how he was hurt?" Mr. Ramsey asked with a quizzical look.

"Yes," Scott grinned, "I think that I can explain it. Perhaps I had better begin at the beginning and tell you the whole story," he added.

Mr. Ramsey was very anxious to get the story, but he saw that Scott was so tired that he could scarcely keep his eyes open. "Better go to bed now. We'll go over the whole thing in the morning and take a party up to rescue Dawson."

They had been talking in the stable. "Is Jed safe here?" he asked anxiously.

"Yes," the supervisor replied, "he's perfectly safe. The town is in no danger. There may be an inch or two of water in the streets in the morning and it may not get here at all. This ground soaks up a tremendous amount of water and the valley is so wide that it cannot amount to much. I am afraid that it will wipe out some of those small ranchers above here."

Scott avoided the curious ones in the hotel lobby who were anxious to hear his story and was soon asleep dreaming of rushing waters and a runaway horse.

CHAPTER XX
THE RESCUE PARTY

Scott was up early the next morning in spite of his strenuous efforts of the day before and Mr. Ramsey met him at the breakfast table.

"Wife's away on a visit," Mr. Ramsey explained, "so I thought I would wait for you and get the story before you had worn it out telling it to these curiosity mongers around here."

Scott told him the whole tale, including Dugan's visit to the cabin the night before he left for the dam. The supervisor listened silently with frowning face. "Sort of a close corporation," he remarked when Scott had finished. "It is certainly remarkable the way you have rounded the whole gang up. It has not been all luck as you say; you have shown very good judgment and done some hard work on it. That ought to put a stop to the monkey business around here for a while. We'll just keep all this information about the graft in the service to ourselves for a while. We are well rid of Dugan and Jed and it will not be much of a trick to dispose of Benson. I think I shall let him stay in the office till it comes time for an investigation and then spring it on him.

"Dawson is the only one that worries me. I believe there is a lot of truth in the story he told you up at the dam. He has made us a mighty good man with the single exception of this dirty business deal in this district of yours, and he certainly has plenty of ability. I have never heard of a smoother scheme than the one he worked. He is more than half right in the argument he put up to you, too. If he really wants to put up a fight, as he probably will, it will be mighty hard to prove the charges against him; especially now that Jed and Dugan are out of it. I am not all sure we can nail him."

"Yes," Scott admitted, "I was counting on Jed pretty strong. It will not be so easy without him and yet I think that I can make out a fairly strong case."

"Think you are not too stiff to ride back up there to the dam to-day?" Mr. Ramsey asked.

"I can make it all right if Jed can travel," Scott said.

"Oh, he's all right. I was out there to see him this morning and he has forgotten all about it. He is certainly a wonderful horse. Well, then, we'll take a couple of the boys from here, including a doctor, and start in about half an hour."

The supervisor went to make his preparations for the trip and Scott hurried out to the stable to see Jed. As Mr. Ramsey had said, he seemed to have forgotten all about it and was all ready to start out again. Scott rubbed him down thoroughly and rode out to meet the supervisor. Jed was a little stiff at first but soon limbered up and insisted on leading the procession.

The mighty flood which had roared so furiously in the cañon up on the mountain had not reached the town at all. It had overflowed the river channel for a short distance but had already receded within its banks. The first ranch above the town had not been touched; the next two or three had been flooded but the water had not gotten into the houses and no damage had been done. In the case of the last two up near the mouth of the cañon it was a different story. Everything movable had been washed away and Bronson's house had been carried from the foundation and was lying on its side far out in the meadow. But no lives had been lost and all the stock had been saved. The settlers considered themselves lucky to have escaped as they did and were very grateful to Scott for the ample warning he had given them.

As they proceeded up the valley the ravages of the flood became more evident. There was a considerable volume of water still coming down the stream bed but the flood was over. It was not till they reached the turn in the valley below the lookout station that the full fury of the rushing water was apparent. The violence of the torrent had carried the water high up on the slope toward the lookout tower and had gouged an enormous pit out of the side of the mountain.

From there on the whole cañon was a total wreck. Not only were all traces of the trail wiped out but the gorge was swept clean. Trees had been torn up by the roots and carried away. What little soil there had been between the rocks was gone and the horses scrambled over slippery beds of smooth, bare rock. An eighth of a mile below the dam they found great chunks of the mason work which had been carried there on the crest of the flood. They began to worry about the safety of the cabin.

The meadow looked more familiar than anything else they had seen. The deep sod alone of all the vegetation in the path of the water had held its own. It was scattered with great chunks of mason work and bowlders and the grass was badly clawed by the wash of the water but it was green and triumphant.

As they rounded the shoulder of rock which hid the view of the dam they heaved a sigh of relief. The west end of the dam, with the little cabin almost on the jagged end of it, was safe. The central portion of the dam was gone completely. Only the encircling crags and mountain peaks looked serenely down on the wreck unchanged. They might wear away eventually but they could withstand many a worse storm than that without showing it.

They hurried to the cabin in search of Dawson. The silence of the place seemed ominous. They found Dawson but he was unconscious and delirious. The suffering and exposure of the day before, the fright of Jed's visit to the cabin and the terrible strain of lying helpless on the very verge of that crumbling dam had been too much for him. In addition to all that the doctor found that he had received a severe blow on the back of the head when he fell. The doctor decided that it would be better to keep him there at the cabin than to try to take him down that slippery trail on a litter and volunteered to stay there and nurse him. It looked as though it would be a close pinch even at that.

Scott explained the situation which had led up to the breaking of the dam and they started back for Benny's. They spread out across the cañon as far as the water had reached and searched every rock and cranny. It was over a quarter of a mile below the dam that they found what they were looking for. High up on the side of the cañon, at the highest point reached by the water, they found the bodies of Dugan and Jed Clark almost locked in each other's arms. It looked as though they had discovered the horrible mistake they had made and were trying to make up for it. The men made litters to carry the bodies down to Benny's where they planned to spend the night. Scott and Mr. Ramsey rode on back to town.

Mr. Ramsey was worried. He wanted to have the investigation and clean out the remnants of the whole ring. This could not be done very well till Dawson was able to be present. It would not be fair to him to have the trial without giving him a chance to defend himself. Moreover, the evidence against him was almost wholly circumstantial and the supervisor doubted very much whether they would be able to convict him on it if he wanted to put up a fight. Knowing Dawson as well as he did he had no doubt about his putting up a fight as long as there was a ghost of a show to win. He had covered up his tracks so carefully that it looked like a very hard thing to prove anything on him. Scott still thought that he could put up a strong case but he did not have any absolute proof.

So the two rode along together in comparative silence, each one worrying over the same problem in his own way. When they rode out of the cañon into the main valley they discovered quite a crowd around the Bronson home. The ranchers from all along the valley had assembled there to try to help Mr. Bronson put his house back on the foundation. These stout-hearted fellows were not in the least discouraged by the catastrophe which had overtaken them. Bronson had suffered more than the others and for that reason they had chosen to help him first. The others had already moved their families back into their homes and the wives were busy cleaning up for a fresh start.

They stopped to speak to the men, and, just as they were leaving, Mr. Bronson led the supervisor aside. "Are you going to be in your office to-morrow morning, Mr. Ramsey?"

"Yes, I expect to be."

"Me and the rest of the boys have something we want to talk over with you, if you'll have the time."

"Come right ahead," Mr. Ramsey urged. He was always glad of an opportunity to coöperate with the settlers in any way and was very popular with them on that account.

"Better come over first thing in the morning," Mr. Ramsey called to Scott as they parted in town, "I want to go over your records and the evidence you have collected. Maybe we can get that out of the way before those ranchers come in."

Scott was kept busy all evening telling the story of the bursting of the dam. Even then he did not satisfy them all and there were so many others waiting to hear it in the morning that he was glad of the excuse to go to the office early. He found the supervisor already there getting together the evidence which he had on hand.

"Looks pretty good, Burton," he said as Scott came in, "but I can't find a thing to prove certainly that Dawson was Jed's partner or was even vitally implicated in this scullduggery in any way. There is no question about it in my mind now but there is no proof which would stand in court."

"I am afraid there isn't," Scott admitted. "I was in hopes that Jed would turn against him, but now that he is gone I can't think of any way to prove it."

Just then there was a tramping of many feet in the hall and the delegation of small ranchers filed into the office. Wren, the big gruff-mannered man who had threatened to thrash Scott for refusing the invitation to dinner when he stopped there to issue a free use permit, was the spokesman.

"I'm not going to take up much of your time," he said in his usual rough way. "I expect you are sort of busy trying to fix up this mess and have mighty little time to talk about anything else. We don't like the idea much of jumping on a man when he is down, but we figure that if we are going to get square with Dawson at all, now is our chance. Moreover, we want to see that justice is done to a friend of ours."

At the mention of getting square with Dawson, Mr. Ramsey pricked up his ears. Possibly there was a chance here to get some evidence from a source on which they had not counted.

"If you gentlemen have any charges to make against Dawson now is certainly the time to make them," he said.

"Well, for the past five years he has been charging us for our free use permits."

"Charging you for them?" the supervisor exclaimed in amazement. "How's that?"

"Don't know how to make it any plainer," Wren answered. "Whenever we took out a free use permit we just had to pay so much for it."

"Why didn't you report it? You knew perfectly well that you did not have to pay for it."

"Hicks thought he knew that one year and all his sheep died. 'Loco weed,' Dawson said."

"And do you mean to say that this thing has been going on regularly on this forest for five years?"

"We never knew what it was to get a free use permit for nothing till this young man here came around this spring. And that's why we are here. We heard that Dawson was trying to put the blame for those extras getting into the forest on him and we are not going to stand for that."

"Have you ever paid money directly to Dawson for this?" Mr. Ramsey asked.

"Not for that, no. That was always paid to the guard or patrolman, but," he hesitated a moment and then continued, "I don't suppose it is much to our credit, but I might as well own up to it if it will help to clean things up; I've paid graft money to him direct for the privilege of running extras on the forest in addition to my free use permit. It was our only chance to get anything for the money he gouged out of us on the permits," he explained.

"How about the rest of you?" the supervisor asked.

"All guilty," responded one of the men.

"Would you be willing to testify to that in court?" the supervisor continued.

"Sure we would. That's what we came for."

"Good," Mr. Ramsey exclaimed, "that will be exactly the proof I am looking for to convict Dawson. I felt sure that he was guilty but could not prove it. I am not fixed to take down that evidence now but I'll come around to see you and get it as soon as I can. I certainly appreciate your help. I don't blame you any for running in your extras under those conditions and I'll forget it."

"Well then," Wren said simply, "I think we'll be going. We have considerable work to do cleaning up around home. Before we go we want to thank this gentleman for the warning he gave us. We treated him pretty shabbily when he first came and now he has paid us back by saving all our stock for us. We feel pretty mean about it and are not ashamed to tell him so."

"Seems to me you have a little more than squared yourselves now," Scott said. "I feel as though I was considerably in your debt."

They all shook hands with Scott cordially and filed out of the office again.

"Things are coming our way, Burton," Mr. Ramsey smiled. "If I could prove that Dawson was Jed Clark's partner now and mixed up with that big deal I would be happy."

"And I can settle that for you," said a familiar voice.

They both turned quickly and Scott recognized the old gentleman whom he had met on the train. He was standing in the doorway and smiling pleasantly.

"I just came into the office," he explained, "and could not help hearing what you said."

The supervisor rose from his chair and greeted the newcomer cordially. "What brings you this far west, Mr. Barnes?" he asked.

"Same thing that's troubling you now, I guess."

"Mr. Barnes," the supervisor said, introducing Scott, "I want you to meet one of our new patrolmen, Mr. Burton. Mr. Barnes," he explained to Scott, "is one of the good sheep men."

"I've met him before," Mr. Barnes said, shaking hands. "Still looking at the country?"

"Yes," Scott answered, "and I find it even more interesting here than it was from the car window."

Mr. Barnes explained to the supervisor how he had come to be acquainted with Scott. "Now about this partnership business. I sold a bunch of sheep to those fellows and they have not finished paying for them. I heard of Jed's death and thought that I better come down here and look into the matter. Can you tell me where I can find Dawson now? I should like to see him to-day if possible."

"Have you heard of the mix up we have had here?" Mr. Ramsey asked.

"No, I only heard that Jed was drowned when the dam went out."

Mr. Ramsey explained the situation. "Now you can see why we would like to have some proof that Dawson was really a partner of Jed's."

"And that, as I said before," answered the old gentleman, "is something which I can prove very easily. I have letters admitting the partnership and notes signed by the two of them."

"Then I guess that settles it. Call Benson, Burton, and I'll finish the job."

"You'll have to call pretty loud," the old gentleman laughed; "he got on the train when I got off."

"Well, it's good riddance to bad rubbish. That ought to finish up the whole gang. I certainly will be glad to get that district clean."

"I'll be glad to produce that evidence any time you want it and I'll see you again before I leave town. Glad to see that you have made good," he added to Scott as he went out.

"Now," said Mr. Ramsey when they were alone once more, "that makes almost a perfect score for you in this business, and

I don't see any reason why I should not recommend you for Dawson's job on the strength of it."

"It is very kind of you to say so and I am certainly glad that you think that way about it, but I would like to wait a little longer till I really learn something about the sheep industry, and moreover I am afraid that it would not be fair to some of the other fellows who have worked just as hard and know a lot more about it than I do. Less than two weeks is rather a short time in which to earn a promotion. If I was altogether a stranger here I would like to try it and feel sure that I could get away with it, but Baxter and some of these other fellows know just how little I know and they would feel that I had been put over them unjustly. It seems to me that Baxter would make a good man for the job. I would like to serve under him as a patrolman for a few months and then if there is a ranger's job open anywhere I would be glad to take it and no one would have any kick coming."

"Some sense in that," Mr. Ramsey agreed. "Of course Baxter is the man who would be directly in line for the appointment if you had not done such especially good work on this deal, and he probably would feel it if you were jumped in ahead of him. If you feel as you say I will recommend Baxter for the ranger's job and send in a report of exceptional ability and extraordinary service for you to the district office, with the recommendation that you be given a ranger's appointment after three months' apprenticeship as a patrolman here on this forest."

"That is exactly what I would like best," Scott said earnestly.

"All right," Mr. Ramsey said, "then that is what I shall do at once."

When Scott rode out of town the next morning he was the happiest man in all the big Southwest. He was carrying a letter of appointment in his pocket for Baxter, he had the assurance that a special letter of recommendation for himself was already on the way to headquarters in Albuquerque, and he had the satisfaction of knowing that he had come West a tenderfoot and had made good; made good in a country where a man is judged on what he has done.

THE END

Lightning Source UK Ltd.
Milton Keynes UK
UKHW010641301220
376134UK00002B/426